Dover Thrift Study Edition

Heart of Darkness

JOSEPH CONRAD

DOVER PUBLICATIONS, INC.
Mineola, New York

Copyright

Bibliographical Note

This Dover edition, first published in 2009, is an republication of the story originally published in the volume *Youth: A Narrative and Two Other Stories* by William Blackwood and Sons, Edinburgh and London in 1902, plus literary analysis and perspectives from *MAXnotes® for Heart of Darkness,* published in 1996 by Research & Education Association, Inc., Piscataway, New Jersey.

Library of Congress Cataloging-in-Publication Data

Conrad, Joseph, 1857–1924.
    Heart of darkness / Joseph Conrad.
        p. cm. — (Dover thrift study edition)
    ISBN-13: 978-0-486-47567-7 (alk. paper)
    ISBN-10: 0-486-47567-0 (alk. paper)
    1. Europeans—Africa—Fiction. 2. Trading posts—Fiction. 3. Degeneration—Fiction. 4. Imperialism—Fiction. 5. Africa—Fiction. 6. Conrad, Joseph, 1857–1924. Heart of darkness. I. Title.

PR6005.O4H4 2009
823'.912—dc22

                                                                    2009026170

Manufactured in the United States by Courier Corporation
47567002
www.doverpublications.com

Publisher's Note

Combining the complete text of a classic novel or drama with a comprehensive study guide, Dover Thrift Study Editions are the most effective way to gain a thorough understanding of the major works of world literature.

The study guide features up-to-date and expert analysis of every chapter or section from the source work. Questions and fully explained answers follow, allowing readers to analyze the material critically. Character lists, author bios, and discussions of the work's historical context are also provided.

Each Dover Thrift Study Edition includes everything a student needs to prepare for homework, discussions, reports, and exams.

Contents

Heart of Darkness

JOSEPH CONRAD

Contents

Heart of Darkness

THE *NELLIE*, A cruising yawl, swung to her anchor without a flutter of the sails, and was at rest. The flood had made, the wind was nearly calm, and being bound down the river, the only thing for it was to come to and wait for the turn of the tide.

The sea-reach of the Thames stretched before us like the beginning of an interminable waterway. In the offing the sea and the sky were welded together without a joint, and in the luminous space the tanned sails of the barges drifting up with the tide seemed to stand still in red clusters of canvas sharply peaked, with gleams of varnished sprits. A haze rested on the low shores that ran out to sea in vanishing flatness. The air was dark above Gravesend, and farther back still seemed condensed into a mournful gloom, brooding motionless over the biggest, and the greatest, town on earth.

The Director of Companies was our captain and our host. We four affectionately watched his back as he stood in the bows looking to seaward. On the whole river there was nothing that looked half so nautical. He resembled a pilot, which to a seaman is trustworthiness personified. It was difficult to realize his work was not out there in the luminous estuary, but behind him, within the brooding gloom. (LONDON)

Between us there was, as I have already said somewhere, the bond of the sea. Besides holding our hearts together through long periods of separation, it had the effect of making us tolerant of each other's yarns—and even convictions. The lawyer—the best of old fellows—had, because of his many years and many virtues, the only cushion on deck, and was lying on the only rug. The accountant had brought out already a box of dominoes, and was toying architecturally with the bones. Marlow sat cross-legged right aft, leaning against the mizzenmast. He had sunken cheeks, a yellow complexion, a straight back, an ascetic aspect, and, with his arms dropped, the palms of hands outwards, resembled an idol. The director, satisfied the anchor had good hold, made his way aft and sat down

1

amongst us. We exchanged a few words lazily. Afterwards there was silence on board the yacht. For some reason or other we did not begin that game of dominoes. We felt meditative, and fit for nothing but placid staring. The day was ending in a serenity of still and exquisite brilliance. The water shone pacifically; the sky, without a speck, was a benign immensity of unstained light; the very mist on the Essex marshes was like a gauzy and radiant fabric, hung from the wooded rises inland, and draping the low shores in diaphanous folds. Only the gloom to the west, brooding over the upper reaches, became more somber every minute, as if angered by the approach of the sun. (LONDON)

And at last, in its curved and imperceptible fall, the sun sank low, and from glowing white changed to a dull red without rays and without heat, as if about to go out suddenly, stricken to death by the touch of that gloom brooding over a crowd of men.

Forthwith a change came over the waters, and the serenity became less brilliant but more profound. The old river in its broad reach rested unruffled at the decline of day, after ages of good service done to the race that peopled its banks, spread out in the tranquil dignity of a waterway leading to the uttermost ends of the earth. We looked at the venerable stream not in the vivid flush of a short day that comes and departs forever, but in the august light of abiding memories. And indeed nothing is easier for a man who has, as the phrase goes, "followed the sea" with reverence and affection, than to evoke the great spirit of the past upon the lower reaches of the Thames. The tidal current runs to and fro in its unceasing service, crowded with memories of men and ships it had borne to the rest of home or to the battles of the sea. It had known and served all the men of whom the nation is proud, from Sir Francis Drake to Sir John Franklin, knights all, titled and untitled—the great knights-errant of the sea. It had borne all the ships whose names are like jewels flashing in the night of time, from the *Golden Hind* returning with her round flanks full of trea-sure, to be visited by the Queen's Highness and thus pass out of the gigantic tale, to the *Erebus* and *Terror*, bound on other conquests—and that never returned. It had known the ships and the men. They had sailed from Deptford, from Greenwich, from Erith—the adventurers and the settlers; kings' ships and the ships of men on 'Change; captains, admirals, the dark "interlopers" of the Eastern trade, and the commissioned "gen-erals" of East India fleets. Hunters for gold or pursuers of fame, they all had gone out on that stream, bearing the sword, and often the torch, messengers of the might within the land, bearers of a spark from the sacred fire. What greatness had not floated on the ebb of that river into the mystery of an unknown earth! . . . The dreams of men, the seed of commonwealths, the germs of empires.

The sun set; the dusk fell on the stream, and lights began to appear along the shore. The Chapman lighthouse, a three-legged thing erect on a mud-flat, shone strongly. Lights of ships moved in the fairway—a great stir of lights going up and going down. And farther west on the upper reaches the place of the monstrous town was still marked ominously on the sky, a brooding gloom in sunshine, a lurid glare under the stars.

"And this also," said Marlow suddenly, "has been one of the dark places of the earth."

He was the only man of us who still "followed the sea." The worst that could be said of him was that he did not represent his class. He was a seaman, but he was a wanderer, too, while most seamen lead, if one may so express it, a sedentary life. Their minds are of the stay-at-home order, and their home is always with them—the ship; and so is their country— the sea. One ship is very much like another, and the sea is always the same. In the immutability of their surroundings the foreign shores, the foreign faces, the changing immensity of life, glide past, veiled not by a sense of mystery but by a slightly disdainful ignorance; for there is nothing mysterious to a seaman unless it be the sea itself, which is the mistress of his existence and as inscrutable as destiny. For the rest, after his hours of work, a casual stroll or a casual spree on shore suffices to unfold for him the secret of a whole continent, and generally he finds the secret not worth knowing. The yarns of seamen have a direct simplicity, the whole meaning of which lies within the shell of a cracked nut. But Marlow was not typical (if his propensity to spin yarns be excepted), and to him the meaning of an episode was not inside like a kernel but outside, enveloping the tale which brought it out only as a glow brings out a haze, in the likeness of one of these misty halos that sometimes are made visible by the spectral illu- mination of moonshine.

His remark did not seem at all surprising. It was just like Marlow. It was accepted in silence. No one took the trouble to grunt even; and presently he said, very slow:

"I was thinking of very old times, when the Romans first came here, nineteen hundred years ago—the other day. . . . Light came out of this river since—you say knights? Yes; but it is like a running blaze on a plain, like a flash of lightning in the clouds. We live in the flicker—may it last as long as the old earth keeps rolling! But darkness was here yesterday. Imagine the feelings of a commander of a fine—what d'ye call 'em?— trireme in the Mediterranean, ordered suddenly to the north; run overland across the Gauls in a hurry; put in charge of one of these craft the legionaries—a wonderful lot of handy men they must have been, too— used to build, apparently by the hundred, in a month or two, if we may believe what we read. Imagine him here—the very end of the world, a sea the color of lead, a sky the color of smoke, a kind of ship about as rigid as a concertina—and going up this river with stores, or orders, or what you like. Sandbanks, marshes, forests, savages—precious little to eat fit for a civilized man, nothing but Thames water to drink. No Falernian wine here, no going ashore. Here and there a military camp lost in a wilderness, like a needle in a bundle of hay—cold, fog, tempests, disease, exile, and death—death skulking in the air, in the water, in the bush. They must have been dying like flies here. Oh, yes—he did it. Did it very well, too, no doubt, and without thinking much about it either, except afterwards to brag of what he had gone through in his time, perhaps. They were men enough to face the darkness. And perhaps he was cheered by keeping his eye on a chance of promotion to the fleet at Ravenna by and by, if he had good friends in Rome and survived the awful climate. Or think of a decent young citizen in a toga—perhaps too much dice, you know—coming out here in the train of some prefect, or tax-gatherer, or trader even, to mend his fortunes. Land in a swamp, march through the woods, and in some inland post feel the savagery, the utter savagery, had closed round him— all that mysterious life of the wilderness that stirs in the forest, in the jungles, in the hearts of wild men. There's no initiation either into such mysteries. He has to live in the midst of the incomprehensible, which is also detestable. And it has a fascination, too, that goes to work upon him. The fascination of the abomination—you know, imagine the growing regrets, the longing to escape, the powerless disgust, the surrender, the hate."

He paused.

"Mind," he began again, lifting one arm from the elbow, the palm of the hand outwards, so that, with his legs folded before him, he had the pose of a Buddha preaching in European clothes and without a lotus flower— "Mind, none of us would feel exactly like this. What saves us is efficiency—the devotion to efficiency. But these chaps were not much account, really. They were no colonists; their administration was merely a squeeze, and nothing more, I suspect. They were conquerors, and for that you want only brute force—nothing to boast of, when you have it, since your strength is just an accident arising from the weakness of others. They grabbed what they could get for the sake of what was to be got. It was just robbery with violence, aggravated murder on a great scale, and men going at it blind—as is very proper for those who tackle a darkness. The conquest of the earth, which mostly means the taking it away from those who have a different complexion or slightly flatter noses than ourselves, is not a pretty thing when you look into it too much. What redeems it is the idea only. An idea at the back of it; not a sentimental pretence but an idea; and an unselfish belief in the idea—something you can set up, and bow down before, and offer a sacrifice to. . . ."

He broke off. Flames glided in the river, small green flames, red flames, white flames, pursuing, overtaking, joining, crossing each other—then separating slowly or hastily. The traffic of the great city went on in the deepening night upon the sleepless river. We looked on, waiting patiently—there was nothing else to do till the end of the flood; but it was only after a long silence, when he said, in a hesitating voice, "I suppose you fellows remember I did once turn fresh-water sailor for a bit," that we knew we were fated, before the ebb began to run, to hear about one of Marlow's inconclusive experiences.

"I don't want to bother you much with what happened to me personally," he began, showing in this remark the weakness of many tellers of tales who seem so often unaware of what their audience would best like to hear; "yet to understand the effect of it on me you ought to know how I got out there, what I saw, how I went up that river to the place where I first met the poor chap. It was the farthest point of navigation and the culminating point of my experience. It seemed somehow to throw a kind of light on everything about me—and into my thoughts. It was somber enough, too—and pitiful—not extraordinary in any way—not very clear either. No, not very clear. And yet it seemed to throw a kind of light.

"I had then, as you remember, just returned to London after a lot of Indian Ocean, Pacific, China Seas—a regular dose of the East—six years or so, and I was loafing about, hindering you fellows in your work and invading your homes, just as though I had got a heavenly mission to civilize you. It was very fine for a time, but after a bit I did get tired of resting. Then I began to look for a ship—I should think the hardest work on earth. But the ships wouldn't even look at me. And I got tired of that game, too.

"Now when I was a little chap I had a passion for maps. I would look for hours at South America, or Africa, or Australia, and lose myself in all the glories of exploration. At that time there were many blank spaces on the earth, and when I saw one that looked particularly inviting on a map (but they all look that) I would put my finger on it and say, 'When I grow up I will go there.' The North Pole was one of these places, I remember. Well, I haven't been there yet, and shall not try now. The glamor's off. Other places were scattered about the Equator, and in every sort of latitude all over the two hemispheres. I have been in some of them, and . . . well, we won't talk about that. But there was one yet—the biggest, the most blank, so to speak—that I had a hankering after.

"True, by this time it was not a blank space any more. It had got filled since my boyhood with rivers and lakes and names. It had ceased to be a blank space of delightful mystery—a white patch for a boy to dream gloriously over. It had become a place of darkness. But there was in it one river especially, a mighty big river, that you could see on the map, resembling an immense snake uncoiled, with its head in the sea, its body at rest curving afar over a vast country, and its tail lost in the depths of the land. And as I looked at the map of it in a shop window, it fascinated me as a snake would a bird—a silly little bird. Then I remembered there was a big concern, a company for trade on that river. Dash it all! I thought to myself, they can't trade without using some kind of craft on that lot of fresh water—steamboats! Why shouldn't I try to get charge of one? I went on along Fleet Street, but could not shake off the idea. The snake had charmed me.

"You understand it was a continental concern, that trading society; but I have a lot of relations living on the continent, because it's cheap and not so nasty as it looks, they say.

"I am sorry to own I began to worry them. This was already a fresh departure for me. I was not used to get things that way, you know. I always went my own road and on my own legs where I had a mind to go. I wouldn't have believed it of myself; but, then—you see—I felt somehow I must get there by hook or by crook. So I worried them. The men said 'My dear fellow,' and did nothing. Then—would you believe it?—I tried the women. I, Charlie Marlow, set the women to work—to get a job. Heavens! Well, you see, the notion drove me. I had an aunt, a dear enthusiastic soul. She wrote: 'It will be delightful. I am ready to do anything, anything for you. It is a glorious idea. I know the wife of a very high personage in the administration, and also a man who has lots of influence with,' etc., etc. She was determined to make no end of fuss to get me appointed skipper of a river steamboat, if such was my fancy.

"I got my appointment—of course; and I got it very quick. It appears the company had received news that one of their captains had been killed in a scuffle with the natives. This was my chance, and it made me the more anxious to go. It was only months and months afterwards, when I made the attempt to recover what was left of the body, that I heard the original quarrel arose from a misunderstanding about some hens. Yes, two black hens. Fresleven—that was the fellow's name, a Dane—thought himself wronged somehow in the bargain, so he went ashore and started to hammer the chief of the village with a stick. Oh, it didn't surprise me in the least to hear this, and at the same time to be told that Fresleven was the gentlest, quietest creature that ever walked on two legs. No doubt he was; but he had been a couple of years already out there engaged in the noble cause, you know, and he probably felt the need at last of asserting his self-respect in some way. Therefore he whacked the old nigger mercilessly, while a big crowd of his people watched him, thunderstruck, till some man—I was told the chief's son—in desperation at hearing the old chap yell, made a tentative jab with a spear at the white man—and of course it went quite easy between the shoulder blades. Then the whole population cleared into the forest, expecting all kinds of calamities to happen, while, on the other hand, the steamer Fresleven commanded left also in a bad panic, in charge of the engineer, I believe. Afterwards nobody seemed to trouble much about Fresleven's remains, till I got out and stepped into his shoes. I couldn't let it rest, though; but when an opportunity offered at last to meet my predecessor, the grass growing through his ribs was tall enough to hide his bones. They were all there. The supernatural being had not been touched after he fell. And the village was deserted, the huts gaped black, rotting, all askew within the fallen enclosures. A calamity had come to it, sure enough. The people had vanished. Mad terror had scattered them, men, women, and children, through the bush, and they had never re-turned. What became of the hens I don't know either. I should think the cause of progress got them, anyhow. However, through this glorious affair I got my appointment, before I had fairly begun to hope for it.

"I flew around like mad to get ready, and before forty-eight hours I was crossing the Channel to show myself to my employers, and sign the contract. In a very few hours I arrived in a city that always makes me think of a whited sepulcher. Prejudice no doubt. I had no difficulty in finding the company's offices. It was the biggest thing in the town, and everybody I met was full of it. They were going to run an oversea empire, and make no end of coin by trade.

"A narrow and deserted street in deep shadow, high houses, innumer-able windows with venetian blinds, a dead silence, grass sprouting be-tween the stones, imposing carriage archways right and left, immense double doors standing ponderously ajar. I slipped through one of these cracks, went up a swept and ungarnished staircase, as arid as a desert, and opened the first door I came to. Two women, one fat and the other slim, sat on straw-bottomed chairs, knitting black wool. The slim one got up and walked straight at me—still knitting with downcast eyes—and only just as I began to think of getting out of her way, as you would for a somnambulist, stood still, and looked up. Her dress was as plain as an umbrella-cover, and she turned round without a word and preceded me into a waiting room. I gave my name, and looked about. Deal table in the middle, plain chairs all round the walls, on one end a large shining map, marked with all the colors of a rainbow. There was a vast amount of red—good to see at any time, because one knows that some real work is done in there, a deuce of a lot of blue, a little green, smears of orange, and, on the East Coast, a purple patch, to show where the jolly pioneers of progress drink the jolly lager beer. However, I wasn't going into any of these. I was going into the yellow. Dead in the center. And the river was there—fascinating—deadly—like a snake. Ough! A door opened, a white-haired secretarial

Congo River

head, but wearing a compassionate expression, appeared, and a skinny forefinger beckoned me into the sanctuary. Its light was dim, and a heavy writing desk squatted in the middle. From behind that structure came out an impression of pale plumpness in a frock coat. The great man himself. He was five feet six, I should judge, and had his grip on the handle-end of ever so many millions. He shook hands, I fancy, murmured vaguely, was satisfied with my French. *Bon voyage*.

"In about forty-five seconds I found myself again in the waiting room with the compassionate secretary, who, full of desolation and sympathy, made me sign some document. I believe I undertook amongst other things not to disclose any trade secrets. Well, I am not going to.

"I began to feel slightly uneasy. You know I am not used to such ceremonies, and there was something ominous in the atmosphere. It was just as though I had been let into some conspiracy—I don't know—something not quite right; and I was glad to get out. In the outer room the two women knitted black wool feverishly. People were arriving, and the younger one was walking back and forth introducing them. The old one sat on her chair. Her flat cloth slippers were propped up on a foot-warmer, and a cat reposed on her lap. She wore a starched white affair on her head, had a wart on one cheek, and silver-rimmed spectacles hung on the tip of her nose. She glanced at me above the glasses. The swift and indifferent placidity of that look troubled me. Two youths with foolish and cheery countenances were being piloted over, and she threw at them the same quick glance of unconcerned wisdom. She seemed to know all about them and about me, too. An eerie feeling came over me. She seemed uncanny and fateful. Often far away there I thought of these two, guarding the door of darkness, knitting black wool as for a warm pall, one introducing, introducing continuously to the unknown, the other scrutinizing the cheery and foolish faces with unconcerned old eyes. *Ave!* Old knitter of black wool. *Morituri te salutant*. Not many of those she looked at ever saw her again—not half, by a long way.

"There was yet a visit to the doctor. 'A simple formality,' assured me the secretary, with an air of taking an immense part in all my sorrows. Accordingly a young chap wearing his hat over the left eyebrow, some clerk I suppose—there must have been clerks in the business, though the house was as still as a house in a city of the dead—came from somewhere upstairs, and led me forth. He was shabby and careless, with inkstains on the sleeves of his jacket, and his cravat was large and billowy, under a chin shaped like the toe of an old boot. It was a little too early for the doctor, so I proposed a drink, and thereupon he developed a vein of joviality. As we sat over our vermouths he glorified the company's business, and by and by I expressed casually my surprise at him not going out there. He became very cool and collected all at once. 'I am not such a fool as I look, quoth Plato to his disciples,' he said sententiously, emptied his glass with great resolution, and we rose.

"The old doctor felt my pulse, evidently thinking of something else the while. 'Good, good for there,' he mumbled, and then with a certain eagerness asked me whether I would let him measure my head. Rather surprised, I said 'yes,' when he produced a thing like calipers and got the dimensions back and front and every way, taking notes carefully. He was an unshaven little man in a threadbare coat like a gaberdine, with his feet in slippers, and I thought him a harmless fool. 'I always ask leave, in the interests of science, to measure the crania of those going out there,' he said. 'And when they come back, too?' I asked. 'Oh, I never see them,' he remarked; 'and, moreover, the changes take place inside, you know.' He smiled, as if at some quiet joke. 'So you are going out there. Famous. Interesting, too.' He gave me a searching glance, and made another note. 'Ever any madness in your family?' he asked, in a matter-of-fact tone. I felt very annoyed. 'Is that question in the interests of science, too?' 'It would be,' he said, without taking notice of my irritation, 'interesting for science to watch the mental changes of individuals, on the spot, but . . .' 'Are you an alienist?' I interrupted. 'Every doctor should be—a little,' answered that original, imperturbably. 'I have a little theory which you messieurs who go out there must help me to prove. This is my share in the advantages my country shall reap from the possession of such a magnificent dependency. The mere wealth I leave to others. Pardon my questions, but you are the first Englishman coming under my observation. . . .' I hastened to assure him I was not in the least typical. 'If I were,' said I, 'I wouldn't be talking like this with you.' 'What you say is rather profound, and probably erroneous,' he said, with a laugh. 'Avoid irritation more than exposure to the sun. Adieu. How do you English say, eh? Good-by. Ah! Good-by. Adieu. In the tropics one must before everything keep calm.' . . . He lifted a warning forefinger. . . . '*Du calme, du calme. Adieu.*'

"One thing more remained to do—say good-by to my excellent aunt. I found her triumphant. I had a cup of tea—the last decent cup of tea for many days—and in a room that most soothingly looked just as you would expect a lady's drawing room to look, we had a long quiet chat by the fireside. In the course of these confidences it became quite plain to me I had been represented to the wife of the high dignitary, and goodness knows to how many more people besides, as an exceptional and gifted creature— a piece of good fortune for the company—a man you don't get hold of every day. Good heavens! and I was going to take charge of a two-penny-half-penny river steamboat with a penny whistle attached! It appeared, however, I was also one of the Workers, with a capital—you know.

Something like an emissary of light, something like a lower sort of apostle. There had been a lot of such rot let loose in print and talk just about that time, and the excellent woman, living right in the rush of all that humbug, got carried off her feet. She talked about 'weaning those ignorant millions from their horrid ways,' till, upon my word, she made me quite uncomfortable. I ventured to hint that the company was run for profit.

" 'You forget, dear Charlie, that the laborer is worthy of his hire,' she said, brightly. It's queer how out of touch with truth women are. They live in a world of their own, and there has never been anything like it, and never can be. It is too beautiful altogether, and if they were to set it up it would go to pieces before the first sunset. Some confounded fact we men have been living contentedly with ever since the day of creation would start up and knock the whole thing over.

"After this I got embraced, told to wear flannel, be sure to write often, and so on—and I left. In the street—I don't know why—a queer feeling came to me that I was an impostor. Odd thing that I, who used to clear out for any part of the world at twenty-four hours' notice, with less thought than most men give to the crossing of a street, had a moment—I won't say of hesitation, but of startled pause, before this commonplace affair. The best way I can explain it to you is by saying that, for a second or two, I felt as though, instead of going to the center of a continent, I were about to set off for the center of the earth.

"I left in a French steamer, and she called in every blamed port they have out there, for, as far as I could see, the sole purpose of landing soldiers and customhouse officers. I watched the coast. Watching a coast as it slips by the ship is like thinking about an enigma. There it is before you—smiling, frowning, inviting, grand, mean, insipid, or savage, and always mute with an air of whispering, Come and find out. This one was almost featureless, as if still in the making, with an aspect of monotonous grimness. The edge of a colossal jungle, so dark-green as to be almost black, fringed with white surf, ran straight, like a ruled line, far, far away along a blue sea whose glitter was blurred by a creeping mist. The sun was fierce, the land seemed to glisten and drip with steam. Here and there grayish-whitish specks showed up clustered inside the white surf, with a flag flying above them perhaps. Settlements some centuries old, and still no bigger than pinheads on the untouched expanse of their background. We pounded along, stopped, landed soldiers; went on, landed customhouse clerks to levy toll in what looked like a God-forsaken wilderness, with a tin shed and a flagpole lost in it; landed more soldiers—to take care of the customhouse clerks, presumably. Some, I heard, got drowned in the surf; but whether they did or not, nobody seemed particularly to care. They were just flung out there, and on we went. Every day the coast looked the same, as though we had not moved; but we passed various places—

trading places—with names like Gran' Bassam, Little Popo; names that seemed to belong to some sordid farce acted in front of a sinister back-cloth. The idleness of a passenger, my isolation amongst all these men with whom I had no point of contact, the oily and languid sea, the uniform somberness of the coast, seemed to keep me away from the truth of things, within the toil of a mournful and senseless delusion. The voice of the surf heard now and then was a positive pleasure, like the speech of a brother. It was something natural, that had its reason, that had a meaning. Now and then a boat from the shore gave one a momentary contact with reality. It was paddled by black fellows. You could see from afar the white of their eyeballs glistening. They shouted, sang; their bodies streamed with per-spiration; they had faces like grotesque masks—these chaps; but they had bone, muscle, a wild vitality, an intense energy of movement, that was as natural and true as the surf along their coast. They wanted no excuse for being there. They were a great comfort to look at. For a time I would feel I belonged still to a world of straightforward facts; but the feeling would not last long. Something would turn up to scare it away. Once, I remember, we came upon a man-of-war anchored off the coast. There wasn't even a shed there, and she was shelling the bush. It appears the French had one of their wars going on thereabouts. Her ensign dropped limp like a rag; the muzzles of the long six-inch guns stuck out all over the low hull; the greasy, slimy swell swung her up lazily and let her down, swaying her thin masts. In the empty immensity of earth, sky, and water, there she was, incompre-hensible, firing into a continent. Pop, would go one of the six-inch guns; a small flame would dart and vanish, a little white smoke would disappear, a tiny projectile would give a feeble screech—and nothing happened. Nothing could happen. There was a touch of insanity in the proceeding, a sense of lugubrious drollery in the sight; and it was not dissipated by somebody on board assuring me earnestly there was a camp of natives—he called them enemies!—hidden out of sight somewhere.

"We gave her her letters (I heard the men in that lonely ship were dying of fever at the rate of three a day) and went on. We called at some more places with farcical names, where the merry dance of death and trade goes on in a still and earthly atmosphere as of an overheated catacomb; all along the formless coast bordered by dangerous surf, as if Nature herself had tried to ward off intruders; in and out of rivers, streams of death in life, whose banks were rotting into mud, whose waters, thickened into slime, invaded the contorted mangroves, that seemed to writhe at us in the extremity of an impotent despair. Nowhere did we stop long enough to get a particularized impression, but the general sense of vague and oppressive wonder grew upon me. It was like a weary pilgrimage amongst hints for nightmares.

"It was upward of thirty days before I saw the mouth of the big river. We anchored off the seat of the government. But my work would not begin till some two hundred miles farther on. So as soon as I could I made a start for a place thirty miles higher up.

"I had my passage on a little seagoing steamer. Her captain was a Swede, and knowing me for a seaman, invited me on the bridge. He was a young man, lean, fair, and morose, with lanky hair and a shuffling gait. As we left the miserable little wharf, he tossed his head contemptuously at the shore. 'Been living there?' he asked. I said, 'Yes.' 'Fine lot these government chaps—are they not?' he went on, speaking English with great precision and considerable bitterness. 'It is funny what some people will do for a few francs a month. I wonder what becomes of that kind when it goes up country?' I said to him I expected to see that soon. 'So-o-o!' he exclaimed. He shuffled athwart, keeping one eye ahead vigilantly. 'Don't be too sure,' he continued. 'The other day I took up a man who hanged himself on the road. He was a Swede, too.' 'Hanged himself! Why, in God's name?' I cried. He kept on looking out watchfully. 'Who knows? The sun too much for him, or the country perhaps.'

"At last we opened a reach. A rocky cliff appeared, mounds of turned-up earth by the shore, houses on a hill, others with iron roofs, amongst a waste of excavations, or hanging to the declivity. A continuous noise of the rapids above hovered over this scene of inhabited devastation. A lot of people, mostly black and naked, moved about like ants. A jetty projected into the river. A blinding sunlight drowned all this at times in a sudden recrudescence of glare. 'There's your company's station,' said the Swede, pointing to three wooden barrack-like structures on the rocky slope. 'I will send your things up. Four boxes did you say? So. Farewell.'

"I came upon a boiler wallowing in the grass, then found a path leading up the hill. It turned aside for the boulders, and also for an undersized railway truck lying there on its back with its wheels in the air. One was off. The thing looked as dead as the carcass of some animal. I came upon more pieces of decaying machinery, a stack of rusty rails. To the left a clump of trees made a shady spot, where dark things seemed to stir feebly. I blinked, the path was steep. A horn tooted to the right, and I saw the black people run. A heavy and dull detonation shook the ground, a puff of smoke came out of the cliff, and that was all. No change appeared on the face of the rock. They were building a railway. The cliff was not in the way or anything; but this objectless blasting was all the work going on.

"A slight clinking behind me made me turn my head. Six black men advanced in a file, toiling up the path. They walked erect and slow, balancing small baskets full of earth on their heads, and the clink kept time with their footsteps. Black rags were wound round their loins, and the short ends behind waggled to and fro like tails. I could see every rib, the joints of their limbs were like knots in a rope; each had an iron collar on his neck, and all were connected together with a chain whose bights swung between them, rhythmically clinking. Another report from the cliff made me think suddenly of that ship of war I had seen firing into a continent. It was the same kind of ominous voice; but these men could by no stretch of imagination be called enemies. They were called criminals, and the outraged law, like the bursting shells, had come to them, an insoluble mystery from the sea. All their meager breasts panted together, the violently dilated nostrils quivered, the eyes stared stonily uphill. They passed me within six inches, without a glance, with that complete, death-like indifference of unhappy savages. Behind this raw matter one of the reclaimed, the product of the new forces at work, strolled despondently, carrying a rifle by its middle. He had a uniform jacket with one button off, and seeing a white man on the path, hoisted his weapon to his shoulder with alacrity. This was simple prudence, white men being so much alike at a distance that he could not tell who I might be. He was speedily reassured, and with a large, white, rascally grin, and a glance at his charge, seemed to take me into partnership in his exalted trust. After all, I also was a part of the great cause of these high and just proceedings.

"Instead of going up, I turned and descended to the left. My idea was to let that chain gang get out of sight before I climbed the hill. You know I am not particularly tender; I've had to strike and to fend off. I've had to resist and to attack sometimes—that's only one way of resisting—without counting the exact cost, according to the demands of such sort of life as I had blundered into. I've seen the devil of violence, and the devil of greed, and the devil of hot desire; but, by all the stars! these were strong, lusty, red-eyed devils, that swayed and drove men—men, I tell you. But as I stood on this hillside, I foresaw that in the blinding sunshine of that land I would become acquainted with a flabby, pretending, weak-eyed devil of a rapacious and pitiless folly. How insidious he could be, too, I was only to find out several months later and a thousand miles farther. For a moment I stood appalled, as though by a warning. Finally I descended the hill, obliquely, towards the trees I had seen.

"I avoided a vast artificial hole somebody had been digging on the slope, the purpose of which I found it impossible to divine. It wasn't a quarry or a sandpit, anyhow. It was just a hole. It might have been connected with the philanthropic desire of giving the criminals something to do. I don't know. Then I nearly fell into a very narrow ravine, almost no more than a scar in the hillside. I discovered that a lot of imported drainage pipes for the settlement had been tumbled in there. There wasn't one that was not broken. It was a wanton smashup. At last I got under the trees. My purpose was to stroll into the shade for a moment; but no sooner within than it seemed to me I had stepped into the gloomy circle of some inferno. The rapids were near, and an uninterrupted, uniform, headlong, rushing noise filled the mournful stillness of the grove, where not a breath stirred, not a leaf moved, with a mysterious sound—as though the tearing pace of the launched earth had suddenly become audible.

"Black shapes crouched, lay, sat between the trees leaning against the trunks, clinging to the earth, half coming out, half effaced within the dim light, in all the attitudes of pain, abandonment, and despair. Another mine on the cliff went off, followed by a slight shudder of the soil under my feet. The work was going on. The work! And this was the place where some of the helpers had withdrawn to die.

"They were dying slowly—it was very clear. They were not enemies, they were not criminals, they were nothing earthly now, nothing but black shadows of disease and starvation, lying confusedly in the greenish gloom. Brought from all the recesses of the coast in all the legality of time contracts, lost in uncongenial surroundings, fed on unfamiliar food, they sickened, became inefficient, and were then allowed to crawl away and rest. These moribund shapes were free as air—and nearly as thin. I began to distinguish the gleam of the eyes under the trees. Then, glancing down, I saw a face near my hand. The black bones reclined at full length with one shoulder against the tree, and slowly the eyelids rose and the sunken eyes looked up at me, enormous and vacant, a kind of blind, white flicker in the depths of the orbs, which died out slowly. The man seemed young—almost a boy—but you know with them it's hard to tell. I found nothing else to do but to offer him one of my good Swede's ship's biscuits I had in my pocket. The fingers closed slowly on it and held—there was no other movement and no other glance. He had tied a bit of white worsted round his neck— Why? Where did he get it? Was it a badge—an ornament—a charm—a propitiatory act? Was there any idea at all connected with it? It looked startling round his black neck, this bit of white thread from beyond the seas.

"Near the same tree two more bundles of acute angles sat with their legs drawn up. One, with his chin propped on his knees, stared at nothing, in an intolerable and appalling manner: his brother phantom rested its forehead, as if overcome with a great weariness; and all about others were scattered in every pose of contorted collapse, as in some picture of a massacre or a pestilence. While I stood horror-struck, one of these creatures rose to his hands and knees, and went off on all fours towards the river to drink. He lapped out of his hand, then sat up in the sunlight, crossing his shins in front of him, and after a time let his wooly head fall on his breastbone.

"I didn't want any more loitering in the shade, and I made haste towards the station. When near the buildings I met a white man, in such an unexpected elegance of getup that in the first moment I took him for a sort of vision. I saw a high starched collar, white cuffs, a light alpaca jacket, snowy trousers, a clear necktie, and varnished boots. No hat. Hair parted, brushed, oiled, under a green-lined parasol held in a big white hand. He was amazing, and had a penholder behind his ear. ACCOUNTANT

"I shook hands with this miracle, and I learned he was the company's chief accountant, and that all the bookkeeping was done at this station. He had come out for a moment, he said, 'to get a breath of fresh air.' The expression sounded wonderfully odd, with its suggestion of sedentary desk life. I wouldn't have mentioned the fellow to you at all, only it was from his lips that I first heard the name of the man who is so indissolubly connected with the memories of that time. Moreover, I respected the fellow. Yes; I respected his collars, his vast cuffs, his brushed hair. His appearance was certainly that of a hairdresser's dummy; but in the great demoralization of the land he kept up his appearance. That's backbone. His starched collars and got-up shirt fronts were achievements of character. He had been out nearly three years; and, later, I could not help asking him how he managed to sport such linen. He had just the faintest blush, and said modestly, 'I've been teaching one of the native women about the station. It was difficult. She had a distaste for the work.' Thus this man had truly accomplished something. And he was devoted to his books, which were in apple-pie order.

"Everything else in the station was in a muddle—heads, things, buildings. Strings of dusty niggers with splay feet arrived and departed; a stream of manufactured goods, rubbishy cottons, beads, and brass wire set into the depths of darkness, and in return came a precious trickle of ivory.

"I had to wait in the station for ten days—an eternity. I lived in a hut in the yard, but to be out of the chaos I would sometimes get into the accountant's office. It was built of horizontal planks, and so badly put together that, as he bent over his high desk, he was barred from neck to heels with narrow strips of sunlight. There was no need to open the big shutter to see. It was hot there, too; big flies buzzed fiendishly, and did not sting, but stabbed. I sat generally on the floor, while, of faultless appearance (and even slightly scented), perching on a high stool, he wrote, he wrote. Sometimes he stood up for exercise. When a truckle bed with a sick man (some invalid agent from upcountry) was put in there, he exhibited a gentle annoyance. 'The groans of this sick person,' he said, 'distract my attention. And without that it is extremely difficult to guard against clerical errors in this climate.'

"One day he remarked, without lifting his head, 'In the interior you will no doubt meet Mr. Kurtz.' On my asking who Mr. Kurtz was, he said he was a first-class agent; and seeing my disappointment at this information, he added slowly, laying down his pen, 'He is a very remarkable person.' Further questions elicited from him that Mr. Kurtz was at present in charge of a trading post, a very important one, in the true ivory-country, at 'the very bottom of there. Sends in as much ivory as all the others put together. . . .' He began to write again. The sick man was too ill to groan. The flies buzzed in a great peace.

"Suddenly there was a growing murmur of voices and a great tramping of feet. A caravan had come in. A violent babble of uncouth sounds burst out on the other side of the planks. All the carriers were speaking together, and in the midst of the uproar the lamentable voice of the chief agent was heard 'giving it up' tearfully for the twentieth time that day. . . . He rose slowly. 'What a frightful row,' he said. He crossed the room gently to look at the sick man, and returning, said to me, 'He does not hear.' 'What! Dead?' I asked, startled. 'No, not yet,' he answered, with great composure. Then, alluding with a toss of the head to the tumult in the station yard, 'When one has got to make correct entries, one comes to hate those savages—hate them to the death.' He remained thoughtful for a moment. 'When you see Mr. Kurtz,' he went on, 'tell him from me that everything here'—he glanced at the desk—'is very satisfactory. I don't like to write to him—with those messengers of ours you never know who may get hold of your letter—at that Central Station.' He stared at me for a moment with his mild, bulging eyes. 'Oh, he will go far, very far,' he began again. 'He will be a somebody in the administration before long. They, above—the council in Europe, you know—mean him to be.'

"He turned to his work. The noise outside had ceased, and presently in going out I stopped at the door. In the steady buzz of flies the homeward-bound agent was lying flushed and insensible; the other, bent over his books, was making correct entries of perfectly correct transactions; and fifty feet below the doorstep I could see the still treetops of the grove of death.

"Next day I left that station at last, with a caravan of sixty men, for a two-hundred-mile tramp.

"No use telling you much about that. Paths, paths, everywhere; a stamped-in network of paths spreading over the empty land, through long grass, through burnt grass, through thickets, down and up chilly ravines, up and down stony hills ablaze with heat; and a solitude, a solitude, nobody, not a hut. The population had cleared out a long time ago. Well, if a lot of mysterious niggers armed with all kinds of fearful weapons suddenly took to traveling on the road between Deal and Gravesend, catching the yokels right and left to carry heavy loads for them, I fancy every farm and cottage thereabouts would get empty very soon. Only here the dwellings were gone, too. Still I passed through several abandoned villages. There's something pathetically childish in the ruins of grass walls. Day after day, with the stamp and shuffle of sixty pair of bare feet behind me, each pair under a sixty-lb. load. Camp, cook, sleep, strike camp, march. Now and then a carrier dead in harness, at rest in the long grass near the path, with an empty water gourd and his long staff lying by his side. A great silence around and above. Perhaps on some quiet night the tremor of far-off drums, sinking, swelling, a tremor vast, faint; a sound weird, appealing, suggestive, and wild—and perhaps with as profound a meaning as the sound of bells in a Christian country. Once a white man in an unbuttoned uniform, camping on the path with an armed escort of lank Zanzibaris, very hospitable and festive—not to say drunk. Was looking after the upkeep of the road he declared. Can't say I saw any road or any upkeep, unless the body of a middle-aged Negro, with a bullethole in the forehead, upon which I absolutely stumbled three miles farther on, may be considered as a permanent improvement. I had a white companion, too, not a bad chap, but rather too fleshy and with the exasperating habit of fainting on the hot hillsides, miles away from the least bit of shade and water. Annoying, you know, to hold your own coat like a parasol over a man's head while he is coming to. I couldn't help asking him once what he meant by coming there at all. 'To make money, of course. What do you think?' he said, scornfully. Then he got fever, and had to be carried in a hammock slung under a pole. As he weighed 224 pounds I had no end of rows with the carriers. They jibbed, ran away, sneaked off with their loads in the night—quite a mutiny. So, one evening, I made a speech in English with gestures, not one of which was lost to the sixty pairs of eyes before me, and the next morning I started the hammock off in front all right. An hour afterwards I came upon the whole concern wrecked in a bush—man, hammock, groans, blankets, horrors. The heavy pole had skinned his poor nose. He was very anxious for me to kill somebody, but there wasn't the shadow of a carrier near. I remember the old doctor, 'It would be interesting for science to watch the mental changes of individuals, on the spot.' I felt I was becoming scientifically interesting. However, all that is to no purpose. On the fifteenth day I came in sight of the big river again, and hobbled into the Central Station. It was on a back water surrounded by scrub and forest, with a pretty border of smelly mud on one side, and on the three others enclosed by a crazy fence of rushes. A neglected gap was all the gate it had, and the first glance at the place was enough to let you see the flabby devil was running that show. White men with long staves in their hands appeared languidly from amongst the buildings, strolling up to take a look at me, and then retired out of sight somewhere. One of them, a stout, excitable chap with black mustaches, informed me with great volubility and many digressions, as soon as I told him who I was, that my steamer was at the bottom of the river. I was thunderstruck. What, how, why? Oh, it was 'all right.' The 'manager himself' was there. All quite correct. 'Everybody had behaved splendidly! splendidly!'—'you must,' he said in agitation, 'go and see the general manager at once. He is waiting!'

"I did not see the real significance of that wreck at once. I fancy I see it now, but I am not sure—not at all. Certainly the affair was too stupid—when I think of it—to be altogether natural. Still . . . But at the moment it presented itself simply as a confounded nuisance. The steamer was sunk. They had started two days before in a sudden hurry up the river with the manager on board, in charge of some volunteer skipper, and before they had been out three hours they tore the bottom out of her on stones, and she sank near the south bank. I asked myself what I was to do there, now my boat was lost. As a matter of fact, I had plenty to do in fishing my command out of the river. I had to set about it the very next day. That, and the repairs when I brought the pieces to the station, took some months.

"My first interview with the manager was curious. He did not ask me to sit down after my twenty-mile walk that morning. He was commonplace in complexion, in feature, in manners, and in voice. He was of middle size and of ordinary build. His eyes, of the usual blue, were perhaps remarkably cold, and he certainly could make his glance fall on one as trenchant and heavy as an axe. But even at these times the rest of his person seemed to disclaim the intention. Otherwise there was only an indefinable, faint expression of his lips, something stealthy—a smile—not a smile—I remember it, but I can't explain. It was unconscious, this smile was, though just after he had said something it got intensified for an instant. It came at the end of his speeches like a seal applied on the words to make the meaning of the commonest phrase appear absolutely inscrutable. He was a common trader, from his youth up employed in these parts—nothing more. He was obeyed, yet he inspired neither love nor fear, nor even respect. He inspired uneasiness. That was it! Uneasiness. Not a definite mistrust—just uneasiness—nothing more. You have no idea how effective such a . . . a . . . faculty can be. He had no genius for organizing, for initiative, or for order even. That was evident in such things as the deplorable state of the station. He had no learning, and no intelligence. His position had come to him—why? Perhaps because he was never ill . . . He had served three terms of three years out there. . . . Because triumphant health in the general rout of constitutions is a kind of power in itself. When he went home on leave he rioted on a large scale—pompously. Jack ashore—with a difference—in externals only. This one could gather from his casual talk. He originated nothing, he could keep the routine going—that's all. But he was great. He was great by this little thing that it was impossible to tell what could control such a man. He never gave that secret away. Perhaps there was nothing within him. Such a suspicion made one pause—for out there there were no external checks. Once when various tropical diseases had laid low almost every 'agent' in the station, he was heard to say, 'Men who come out here should have no entrails.' He sealed the utterance with that smile of his, as though it had been a door opening into a darkness he had in his keeping. You fancied you had seen things—but the seal was on. When annoyed at mealtimes by the constant quarrels of the white men about precedence, he ordered an immense round table to be made, for which a special house had to be built. This was the station's messroom. Where he sat was the first place—the rest were nowhere. One felt this to be his unalterable conviction. He was neither civil nor uncivil. He was quiet. He allowed his 'boy'—an overfed young Negro from the coast—to treat the white men, under his very eyes, with provoking insolence.

"He began to speak as soon as he saw me. I had been very long on the road. He could not wait. Had to start without me. The up-river stations had to be relieved. There had been so many delays already that he did not know who was dead and who was alive, and how they got on—and so on, and so on. He paid no attention to my explanations, and, playing with a stick of sealing wax, repeated several times that the situation was 'very grave, very grave.' There were rumors that a very important station was in jeopardy, and its chief, Mr. Kurtz, was ill. Hoped it was not true. Mr. Kurtz was . . . I felt weary and irritable. Hang Kurtz, I thought. I interrupted him by saying I had heard of Mr. Kurtz on the coast. 'Ah! So they talk of him down there,' he murmured to himself. Then he began again, assuring me Mr. Kurtz was the best agent he had, an exceptional man, of the greatest importance to the company; therefore I could understand his anxiety. He was, he said, 'very, very uneasy.' Certainly he fidgeted on his chair a good deal, exclaimed, 'Ah, Mr. Kurtz!' broke the stick of sealing wax and seemed dumfounded by the accident. Next thing he wanted to know 'how long it would take to' . . . I interrupted him again. Being hungry, you know, and kept on my feet, too, I was getting savage. 'How could I tell?' I said. 'I hadn't even seen the wreck yet—some months, no doubt.' All this talk seemed to me so futile. 'Some months,' he said. 'Well, let us say three months before we can make a start. Yes. That ought to do the affair.' I flung out of his hut (he lived all alone in a clay hut with a sort of veranda) muttering to myself my opinion of him. He was a chattering idiot. Afterwards I took it back when it was borne in upon me startlingly with what extreme nicety he had estimated the time requisite for the 'affair.'

"I went to work the next day, turning, so to speak, my back on that station. In that way only it seemed to me I could keep my hold on the redeeming facts of life. Still, one must look about sometimes; and then I saw this station, these men strolling aimlessly about in the sunshine of the yard. I asked myself sometimes what it all meant. They wandered here and there with their absurd long staves in their hands, like a lot of faithless pilgrims bewitched inside a rotten fence. The word 'ivory' rang in the air, was whispered, was sighed. You would think they were praying to it. A taint of imbecile rapacity blew through it all, like a whiff from some corpse. By Jove! I've never seen anything so unreal in my life. And outside, the silent wilderness surrounding this cleared speck on the earth struck me as something great and invincible, like evil or truth, waiting patiently for the passing away of this fantastic invasion.

"Oh, these months! Well, never mind. Various things happened. One evening a grass shed full of calico, cotton prints, beads, and I don't know what else, burst into a blaze so suddenly that you would have thought the earth had opened to let an avenging fire consume all that trash. I was smoking my pipe quietly by my dismantled steamer, and saw them all cutting capers in the light, with their arms lifted high, when the stout man with mustaches came tearing down to the river, a tin pail in his hand, assured me that everybody was 'behaving splendidly, splendidly,' dipped about a quart of water and tore back again. I noticed there was a hole in the bottom of his pail.

"I strolled up. There was no hurry. You see the thing had gone off like a box of matches. It had been hopeless from the very first. The flame had leaped high, driven everybody back, lighted up everything—and collapsed. The shed was already a heap of embers glowing fiercely. A nigger was being beaten near by. They said he had caused the fire in some way; be that as it may, he was screeching most horribly. I saw him, later, for several days, sitting in a bit of shade looking very sick and trying to recover himself: afterwards he arose and went out—and the wilderness without a sound took him into its bosom again. As I approached the glow from the dark I found myself at the back of two men, talking. I heard the name of Kurtz pronounced, then the words, 'take advantage of this unfortunate accident.' One of the men was the manager. I wished him a good evening. 'Did you ever see anything like it—eh? It is incredible,' he said, and walked off. The other man remained. He was a first-class agent, young, gentlemanly, a bit reserved, with a forked little beard and a hooked nose. He was standoffish with the other agents, and they on their side said he was the manager's spy upon them. As to me, I had hardly ever spoken to him before. We got into talk, and by and by we strolled away from the hissing ruins. Then he asked me to his room, which was in the main building of the station. He struck a match, and I perceived that this young aristocrat had not only a silver-mounted dressing case but also a whole candle all to himself. Just at that time the manager was the only man supposed to have any right to candles. Native mats covered the clay walls; a collection of spears, assagais, shields, knives was hung up in trophies. The business intrusted to this fellow was the making of bricks—so I had been informed; but there wasn't a fragment of a brick anywhere in the station, and he had been there more than a year—waiting. It seems he could not make bricks without something, I don't know what—straw maybe. Anyways, it could not be found there, and as it was not likely to be sent from Europe, it did not appear clear to me what he was waiting for. An act of special creation perhaps. However, they were all waiting—all the sixteen or twenty pilgrims of them—for something; and upon my word it did not seem an uncongenial occupation, from the way they took it, though the only thing that ever came to them was disease—as far as I could see. They beguiled the time by backbiting and intriguing against each other in a foolish kind of way. There was an air of plotting about that station, but nothing came of it, of course. It was as unreal as everything else—as the philanthropic pretense of the whole concern, as their talk, as their government, as their show of work. The only real feeling was a desire to get appointed to a trading post where ivory was to be had, so that they could earn percentages. They intrigued and slandered and hated each other only on that account, but as to effectually lifting a little finger—oh, no. By heavens! There is something after all in the world allowing one man to steal a horse while another must not look at a halter. Steal a horse straight out. Very well. He has done it. Perhaps he can ride. But there is a way of looking at a halter that would provoke the most charitable of saints into a kick.

"I had no idea why he wanted to be sociable, but as we chatted in there it suddenly occurred to me the fellow was trying to get at something—in fact, pumping me. He alluded constantly to Europe, to the people I was supposed to know there—putting leading questions as to my acquaintances in the sepulchral city, and so on. His little eyes glittered like mica discs—with curiosity—though he tried to keep up a bit of superciliousness. At first I was astonished, but very soon I became awfully curious to see what he would find out from me. I couldn't possibly imagine what I had in me to make it worth his while. It was very pretty to see how he baffled himself, for in truth my body was full only of chills, and my head had nothing in it but that wretched steamboat business. It was evident he took me for a perfectly shameless prevaricator. At last he got angry, and, to conceal a movement of furious annoyance, he yawned. I rose. Then I noticed a small sketch in oils, on a panel, representing a woman, draped and blindfolded, carrying a lighted torch. The background was somber—

almost black. The movement of the woman was stately, and the effect of the torchlight on the face was sinister.

"It arrested me, and he stood by civilly, holding an empty half-pint champagne bottle (medical comforts) with the candle stuck in it. To my question he said Mr. Kurtz had painted this—in this very station more than a year ago—while waiting for means to go to his trading post. 'Tell me, pray,' said I, 'who is this Mr. Kurtz?'

"'The chief of the Inner Station,' he answered in a short tone, looking away. 'Much obliged,' I said, laughing. 'And you are the brickmaker of the Central Station. Everyone knows that.' He was silent for a while. 'He is a prodigy,' he said at last. 'He is an emissary of pity, and science, and progress, and devil knows what else. We want,' he began to declaim suddenly, 'for the guidance of the cause intrusted to us by Europe, so to speak, higher intelligence, wide sympathies, a singleness of purpose.' 'Who says that?' I asked. 'Lots of them,' he replied. 'Some even write that; and so *he* comes here, a special being, as you ought to know.' 'Why ought I to know?' I interrupted, really surprised. He paid no attention. 'Yes. Today he is chief of the best station, next year he will be assistant manager, two years more and . . . but I daresay you know what he will be in two years' time. You are of the new gang—the gang of virtue. The same people who sent him specially also recommended you. Oh, don't say no. I've my own eyes to trust.' Light dawned upon me. My dear aunt's influential acquaintances were producing an unexpected effect upon that young man. I nearly burst into a laugh. 'Do you read the company's confidential correspondence?' I asked. He hadn't a word to say. It was great fun. 'When Mr. Kurtz,' I continued, severely, 'is general manager, you won't have the opportunity.'

"He blew the candle out suddenly, and we went outside. The moon had risen. Black figures strolled about listlessly, pouring water on the glow, whence proceeded a sound of hissing; steam ascended in the moonlight, the beaten nigger groaned somewhere. 'What a row the brute makes!' said the indefatigable man with the mustaches, appearing near us. 'Serve him right. Transgression—punishment—bang! Pitiless, pitiless. That's the only way. This will prevent all conflagrations for the future. I was just telling the manager . . .' He noticed my companion, and became crestfallen all at once. 'Not in bed yet,' he said, with a kind of servile heartiness; 'it's so natural. Ha! Danger—agitation.' He vanished. I went on to the river side, and the other followed me. I heard a scathing murmur at my ear, 'Heap of muffs—go to.' The pilgrims could be seen in knots gesticulating, discussing. Several had still their staves in their hands. I truly believe they took these sticks to bed with them. Beyond the fence the forest stood up spectrally in the moonlight, and through the dim stir, through the faint sounds of that lamentable courtyard, the silence of the land went home to one's very heart—its mystery, its greatness, the amazing reality of its concealed life. The hurt nigger moaned feebly somewhere near by, and then fetched a deep sigh that made me mend my pace away from there. I felt a hand introducing itself under my arm. 'My dear sir,' said the fellow, 'I don't want to be misunderstood, and especially by you, who will see Mr. Kurtz long before I can have that pleasure. I wouldn't like him to get a false idea of my disposition. . . .' *[handwritten marginal note: devil spirit to who found...]*

"I let him run on, this papier-mâché Mephistopheles, and it seemed to me that if I tried I could poke my forefinger through him, and would find nothing inside but a little loose dirt, maybe. He, don't you see, had been planning to be assistant manager by and by under the present man, and I could see that the coming of that Kurtz had upset them both not a little. He talked precipitately, and I did not try to stop him. I had my shoulders against the wreck of my steamer, hauled up on the slope like a carcass of some big river animal. The smell of mud, of primeval mud, by Jove! was in my nostrils, the high stillness of primeval forest was before my eyes; there were shiny patches on the black creek. The moon had spread over everything a thin layer of silver—over the rank grass, over the mud, upon the wall of matted vegetation standing higher than the wall of a temple, over the great river I could see through a somber gap glittering, glittering, as it flowed broadly by without a murmur. All this was great, expectant, mute, while the man jabbered about himself. I wondered whether the stillness on the face of the immensity looking at us two were meant as an appeal or as a menace. What were we who had strayed in here? Could we handle that dumb thing, or would it handle us? I felt how big, how confoundedly big, was that thing that couldn't talk, and perhaps was deaf as well. What was in there? I could see a little ivory coming out from there, and I had heard Mr. Kurtz was in there. I had heard enough about it, too—God knows! Yet somehow it didn't bring any image with it—no more than if I had been told an angel or a fiend was in there. I believed it in the same way one of you might believe there are inhabitants in the planet Mars. I knew once a Scotch sailmaker who was certain, dead sure, there were people in Mars. If you asked him for some idea how they looked and behaved, he would get shy and mutter something about 'walking on all fours.' If you as much as smiled, he would—though a man of sixty—offer to fight you. I would not have gone so far as to fight for Kurtz, but I went for him near enough to a lie. You know I hate, detest, and can't bear a lie, not because I am straighter than the rest of us, but simply because it appalls me. There is a taint of death, a flavor of mortality in lies—which is exactly what I hate and detest in the world—what I want to forget. It makes me miserable and sick, like biting something rotten would do. Temperament, I suppose.

Well, I went near enough to it by letting the young fool there believe anything he liked to imagine as to my influence in Europe. I became in an instant as much of a pretense as the rest of the bewitched pilgrims. This simply because I had a notion it somehow would be of help to that Kurtz whom at the time I did not see—you understand. He was just a word for me. I did not see the man in the name any more than you do. Do you see him? Do you see the story? Do you see anything? It seems to me I am trying to tell you a dream—making a vain attempt, because no relation of a dream can convey the dream-sensation, that commingling of absurdity, surprise, and bewilderment in a tremor of struggling revolt, that notion of being captured by the incredible which is of the very essence of dreams. . . ."

He was silent for a while.

". . . No, it is impossible; it is impossible to convey the life-sensation of any given epoch of one's existence—that which makes its truth, its meaning—its subtle and penetrating essence. It is impossible. We live, as we dream—alone. . . ."

He paused again as if reflecting, then added:

"Of course in this you fellows see more than I could then. You see me, whom you know. . . ."

It had become so pitch dark that we listeners could hardly see one another. For a long time already he, sitting apart, had been no more to us than a voice. There was not a word from anybody. The others might have been asleep, but I was awake. I listened, I listened on the watch for the sentence, for the word, that would give me the clue to the faint uneasiness inspired by this narrative that seemed to shape itself without human lips in the heavy night air of the river.

". . . Yes—I let him run on," Marlow began again, "and think what he pleased about the powers that were behind me. I did! And there was nothing behind me! There was nothing but that wretched, old, mangled steamboat I was leaning against, while he talked fluently about 'the necessity for every man to get on.' 'And when one comes out here, you conceive, it is not to gaze at the moon.' Mr. Kurtz was a 'universal genius,' but even a genius would find it easier to work with 'adequate tools—intelligent men.' He did not make bricks—why, there was a physical impossibility in the way—as I was well aware; and if he did secretarial work for the manager, it was because 'no sensible man rejects wantonly the confidence of his superiors.' Did I see it? I saw it. What more did I want? What I really wanted was rivets, by heaven! Rivets. To get on with the work—to stop the hole. Rivets I wanted. There were cases of them down at the coast—cases—piled up—burst—split! You kicked a loose rivet at every second step in that station yard on the hillside. Rivets had rolled into the grove of death. You could fill your pockets with rivets for the trouble of stooping down—and there wasn't one rivet to be found where it was wanted. We had plates that would do, but nothing to fasten them with. And every week the messenger, a lone Negro, letter bag on shoulder and staff in hand, left our station for the coast. And several times a week a coast caravan came in with trade goods—ghastly glazed calico that made you shudder only to look at it, glass beads, value about a penny a quart, confounded spotted cotton handkerchiefs. And no rivets. Three carriers could have brought all that was wanted to set that steamboat afloat.

"He was becoming confidential now, but I fancy my unresponsive attitude must have exasperated him at last, for he judged it necessary to inform me he feared neither God nor devil, let alone any mere man. I said I could see that very well, but what I wanted was a certain quantity of rivets—and rivets were what really Mr. Kurtz wanted, if he had only known it. Now letters went to the coast every week. . . . 'My dear sir,' he cried, 'I write from dictation.' I demanded rivets. There was a way—for an intelligent man. He changed his manner; became very cold, and suddenly began to talk about a hippopotamus; wondered whether sleeping on board the steamer (I stuck to my salvage night and day) I wasn't disturbed. There was an old hippo that had the bad habit of getting out on the bank and roaming at night over the station grounds. The pilgrims used to turn out in a body and empty every rifle they could lay hands on at him. Some even had sat up o' nights for him. All this energy was wasted, though. 'That animal has a charmed life,' he said; 'but you can say this only of brutes in this country. No man—you apprehend me?—no man here bears a charmed life.' He stood there for a moment in the moonlight with his delicate hooked nose set a little askew, and his mica eyes glittering without a wink, then, with a curt good night, he strode off. I could see he was disturbed and considerably puzzled, which made me feel more hopeful than I had been for days. It was a great comfort to turn from that chap to my influential friend, the battered, twisted, ruined, tinpot steamboat. I clambered on board. She rang under my feet like an empty Huntley and Palmer biscuit tin kicked along a gutter; she was nothing so solid in make, and rather less pretty in shape, but I had expended enough hard work on her to make me love her. No influential friend would have served me better. She had given me a chance to come out a bit—to find out what I could do. No, I don't like work. I had rather laze about and think of all the fine things that can be done. I don't like work—no man does—but I like what is in the work, the chance to find yourself. Your own reality—for yourself, not for others—what no other man can ever know. They can only see the mere show, and never can tell what it really means.

"I was not surprised to see somebody sitting aft, on the deck, with his

legs dangling over the mud. You see I rather chummed with the few
mechanics there were in that station, whom the other pilgrims naturally
despised—on account of their imperfect manners, I suppose. This was the
foreman—a boilermaker by trade—a good worker. He was a lank, bony,
yellow-faced man, with big intense eyes. His aspect was worried, and his
head was as bald as the palm of my hand; but his hair in falling seemed to
have stuck to his chin, and had prospered in the new locality, for his beard
hung down to his waist. He was a widower with six young children (he had
left them in charge of a sister of his to come out there), and the passion of
his life was pigeon flying. He was an enthusiast and a connoisseur. He
would rave about pigeons. After work hours he used sometimes to come
over from his hut for a talk about his children and his pigeons; at work,
when he had to crawl in the mud under the bottom of the steamboat, he
would tie up that beard of his in a kind of white serviette he brought for the
purpose. It had loops to go over his ears. In the evening he could be seen
squatted on the bank rinsing that wrapper in the creek with great care,
then spreading it solemnly on a bush to dry.

"I slapped him on the back and shouted 'We shall have rivets!' He
scrambled to his feet exclaiming 'No! Rivets!' as though he couldn't
believe his ears. Then in a low voice, 'You . . . eh?' I don't know why we
behaved like lunatics. I put my finger to the side of my nose and nodded
mysteriously. 'Good for you!' he cried, snapped his fingers above his head,
lifting one foot. I tried a jig. We capered on the iron deck. A frightful
clatter came out of that hulk, and the virgin forest on the other bank of the
creek sent it back in a thundering roll upon the sleeping station. It must
have made some of the pilgrims sit up in their hovels. A dark figure
obscured the lighted doorway of the manager's hut, vanished, then, a
second or so after, the doorway itself vanished, too. We stopped, and the
silence driven away by the stamping of our feet flowed back again from the
recesses of the land. The great wall of vegetation, an exuberant and
entangled mass of trunks, branches, leaves, boughs, festoons, motionless
in the moonlight, was like a rioting invasion of soundless life, a rolling
wave of plants, piled up, crested, ready to topple over the creek, to sweep
every little man of us out of his little existence. And it moved not. A
deadened burst of mighty splashes and snorts reached us from afar, as
though an ichthyosaurus had been taking a bath of glitter in the great river.
'After all,' said the boilermaker in a reasonable tone, 'why shouldn't we get
the rivets?' Why not, indeed! I did not know of any reason why we
shouldn't. 'They'll come in three weeks,' I said, confidently.

"But they didn't. Instead of rivets there came an invasion, an infliction,
a visitation. It came in sections during the next three weeks, each section
headed by a donkey carrying a white man in new clothes and tan shoes,

bowing from that elevation right and left to the impressed pilgrims. A quarrelsome band of footsore sulky niggers trod on the heels of the donkey; a lot of tents, campstools, tin boxes, white cases, brown bales would be shot down in the courtyard, and the air of mystery would deepen a little over the muddle of the station. Five such instalments came, with their absurd air of disorderly flight with the loot of innumerable outfit shops and provision stores, that, one would think, they were lugging, after a raid, into the wilderness for equitable division. It was an inextricable mess of things decent in themselves but that human folly made look like spoils of thieving.

"This devoted band called itself the Eldorado Exploring Expedition, and I believe they were sworn to secrecy. Their talk, however, was the talk of sordid buccaneers: it was reckless without hardihood, greedy without audacity, and cruel without courage; there was not an atom of foresight or of serious intention in the whole batch of them, and they did not seem aware these things are wanted for the work of the world. To tear treasure out of the bowels of the land was their desire, with no more moral purpose at the back of it than there is in burglars breaking into a safe. Who paid the expenses of the noble enterprise I don't know; but the uncle of our manager was leader of that lot.

"In exterior he resembled a butcher in a poor neighborhood, and his eyes had a look of sleepy cunning. He carried his fat paunch with ostentation on his short legs, and during the time his gang infested the station spoke to no one but his nephew. You could see these two roaming about all day long with their heads close together in an everlasting confab.

"I had given up worrying myself about the rivets. One's capacity for that kind of folly is more limited than you would suppose. I said Hang!—and let things slide. I had plenty of time for meditation, and now and then I would give some thought to Kurtz. I wasn't very interested in him. No. Still, I was curious to see whether this man, who had come out equipped with moral ideas of some sort, would climb to the top after all and how he would set about his work when there."

II

"One evening as I was lying flat on the deck of my steamboat, I heard voices approaching—and there were the nephew and the uncle strolling along the bank. I laid my head on my arm again, and had nearly lost myself in a doze, when somebody said in my ear, as it were: 'I am as harmless as a little child, but I don't like to be dictated to. Am I the manager—or am I not? I was ordered to send him there. It's incredible.' . . . I became aware that the two were standing on the shore alongside the forepart of the steamboat, just below my head. I did not move; it did not occur to me to move: I was sleepy. 'It *is* unpleasant,' grunted the uncle. 'He has asked the administration to be sent there,' said the other, 'with the idea of showing what he could do; and I was instructed accordingly. Look at the influence that man must have. Is it not frightful?' They both agreed it was frightful, then made several bizarre remarks: 'Make rain and fine weather—one man—the council—by the nose'—bits of absurd sentences that got the better of my drowsiness, so that I had pretty near the whole of my wits about me when the uncle said, 'The climate may do away with this difficulty for you. Is he alone there?' 'Yes,' answered the manager; 'he sent his assistant down the river with a note to me in these terms: "Clear this poor devil out of the country, and don't bother sending more of that sort. I had rather be alone than have the kind of men you can dispose of with me." It was more than a year ago. Can you imagine such impudence!' 'Anything since then?' asked the other, hoarsely. 'Ivory,' jerked the nephew; 'lots of it—prime sort—lots—most annoying, from him.' 'And with that?' questioned the heavy rumble. 'Invoice,' was the reply fired out, so to speak. Then silence. They had been talking about Kurtz.

"I was broad awake by this time, but, lying perfectly at ease, remained still, having no inducement to change my position. 'How did that ivory come all this way?' growled the elder man, who seemed very vexed. The other explained that it had come with a fleet of canoes in charge of an English half-caste clerk Kurtz had with him; that Kurtz had apparently intended to return himself, the station being by that time bare of goods and stores, but after coming three hundred miles, had suddenly decided to go back, which he started to do alone in a small dugout with four paddlers, leaving the half-caste to continue down the river with the ivory. The two fellows there seemed astounded at anybody attempting such a thing. They were at a loss for an adequate motive. As to me, I seemed to see Kurtz for the first time. It was a distinct glimpse: the dugout, four paddling savages, and the lone white man turning his back suddenly on the headquarters, on relief, on thoughts of home—perhaps; setting his face towards the depths of the wilderness, towards his empty and desolate station. I did not know the motive. Perhaps he was just simply a fine fellow who stuck to his work for its own sake. His name, you understand, had not been pronounced once. He was 'that man.' The half-caste, who, as far as I could see, had conducted a difficult trip with great prudence and pluck, was invariably alluded to as 'that scoundrel.' The 'scoundrel' had reported that the 'man' had been very ill—had recovered imperfectly. . . . The two below me moved away then a few paces, and strolled back and forth at some little distance. I heard: 'Military post—doctor—two hundred miles—quite alone now—unavoidable delays—nine months—no news—strange rumors.' They approached again, just as the manager was saying, 'No one, as far as I know, unless a species of wandering trader—a pestilential fellow, snapping ivory from the natives.' Who was it they were talking about now? I gathered in snatches that this was some man supposed to be in Kurtz's district, and of whom the manager did not approve. 'We will not be free from unfair competition till one of these fellows is hanged for an example,' he said. 'Certainly,' grunted the other; 'get him hanged! Why not? Anything—anything can be done in this country. That's what I say; nobody here, you understand, *here*, can endanger your position. And why? You stand the climate—you outlast them all. The danger is in Europe; but there before I left I took care to—' They moved off and whispered, then their voices rose again. 'The extraordinary series of delays is not my fault. I did my best.' The fat man sighed. 'Very sad.' 'And the pestiferous absurdity of his talk,' continued the other; 'he bothered me enough when he was here. "Each station should be like a beacon on the road towards better things, a center for trade of course, but also for humanizing, improving, instructing." Conceive you—that ass! And he wants to be manager! No, it's—' Here he got choked by excessive indignation, and I lifted my head the least bit. I was surprised to see how near they were— right under me. I could have spat upon their hats. They were looking on the ground, absorbed in thought. The manager was switching his leg with a slender twig; his sagacious relative lifted his head. 'You have been well since you came out this time?' he asked. The other gave a start. 'Who? I? Oh! Like a charm—like a charm. But the rest—oh, my goodness! All sick. They die so quick, too, that I haven't the time to send them out of the country—it's incredible!' 'H'm. Just so,' grunted the uncle. 'Ah! my boy, trust to this—I say, trust to this.' I saw him extend his short flipper of an arm for a gesture that took in the forest, the creek, the mud, the river— seemed to beckon with a dishonoring flourish before the sunlit face of the land a treacherous appeal to the lurking death, to the hidden evil, to the profound darkness of its heart. It was so startling that I leaped to my feet and looked back at the edge of the forest, as though I had expected an answer of some sort to that black display of confidence. You know the foolish notions that come to one sometimes. The high stillness confronted these two figures with its ominous patience, waiting for the passing away of a fantastic invasion.

"They swore aloud together—out of sheer fright, I believe—then pretending not to know anything of my existence, turned back to the station. The sun was low; and leaning forward side by side, they seemed to be tugging painfully uphill their two ridiculous shadows of unequal length, that trailed behind them slowly over the tall grass without bending a single blade.

"In a few days the Eldorado Expedition went into the patient wilderness, that closed upon it as the sea closes over a diver. Long afterwards the news came that all the donkeys were dead. I know nothing as to the fate of the less valuable animals. They, no doubt, like the rest of us, found what they deserved. I did not inquire. I was then rather excited at the prospect of meeting Kurtz very soon. When I say very soon I mean it comparatively. It was just two months from the day we left the creek when we came to the bank below Kurtz's station.

"Going up that river was like traveling back to the earliest beginnings of the world, when vegetation rioted on the earth and the big trees were kings. An empty stream, a great silence, an impenetrable forest. The air was warm, thick, heavy, sluggish. There was no joy in the brilliance of sunshine. The long stretches of the waterway ran on, deserted, into the gloom of overshadowed distances. On silvery sandbanks hippos and alligators sunned themselves side by side. The broadening waters flowed through a mob of wooded islands; you lost your way on that river as you would in a desert, and butted all day long against shoals, trying to find the channel, till you thought yourself bewitched and cut off forever from everything you had known once—somewhere—far away—in another existence perhaps. There were moments when one's past came back to one, as it will sometimes when you have not a moment to spare to yourself; but it came in the shape of an unrestful and noisy dream, remembered with wonder amongst the overwhelming realities of this strange world of plants, and water, and silence. And this stillness of life did not in the least resemble a peace. It was the stillness of an implacable force brooding over an inscrutable intention. It looked at you with a vengeful aspect. I got used to it afterwards; I did not see it any more; I had no time. I had to keep guessing at the channel; I had to discern, mostly by inspiration, the signs of hidden banks; I watched for sunken stones; I was learning to clap my teeth smartly before my heart flew out, when I shaved by a fluke some infernal sly old snag that would have ripped the life out of the tin-pot steamboat and drowned all the pilgrims; I had to keep a lookout for the signs of dead wood we could cut up in the night for next day's steaming. When you have to attend to things of that sort, to the mere incidents of the surface, the reality—the reality, I tell you—fades. The inner truth is hidden—luckily, luckily. But I felt it all the same; I felt often its mysterious stillness watching me at my monkey tricks, just as it watches you fellows performing on your respective tightropes for—what is it? a half crown a tumble—"

"Try to be civil, Marlow," growled a voice, and I knew there was at least one listener awake besides myself.

"I beg your pardon. I forgot the heartache which makes up the rest of the price. And indeed what does the price matter, if the trick be well done?

You do your tricks very well. And I didn't do badly either, since I managed not to sink that steamboat on my first trip. It's a wonder to me yet. Imagine a blindfolded man set to drive a van over a bad road. I sweated and shivered over that business considerably, I can tell you. After all, for a seaman, to scrape the bottom of the thing that's supposed to float all the time under his care is the unpardonable sin. No one may know of it, but you never forget the thump—eh? A blow on the very heart. You remember it, you dream of it, you wake up at night and think of it—years after—and go hot and cold all over. I don't pretend to say that steamboat floated all the time. More than once she had to wade for a bit, with twenty cannibals splashing around and pushing. We had enlisted some of these chaps on the way for a crew. Fine fellows—cannibals—in their place. They were men one could work with, and I am grateful to them. And, after all, they did not eat each other before my face: they had brought along a provision of hippo meat which went rotten, and made the mystery of the wilderness stink in my nostrils. Phoo! I can sniff it now. I had the manager on board and three or four pilgrims with their staves—all complete. Sometimes we came upon a station close by the bank, clinging to the skirts of the unknown, and the white men rushing out of a tumbledown hovel, with great gestures of joy and surprise and welcome, seemed very strange—had the appearance of being held there captive by a spell. The word ivory would ring in the air for a while—and on we went again into the silence, along empty reaches, round the still bends, between the high walls of our winding way, reverberating in hollow claps the ponderous beat of the stern wheel. Trees, trees, millions of trees, massive, immense, running up high; and at their foot, hugging the bank against the stream, crept the little begrimed steamboat, like a sluggish beetle crawling on the floor of a lofty portico. It made you feel very small, very lost, and yet it was not altogether depressing, that feeling. After all, if you were small, the grimy beetle crawled on—which was just what you wanted it to do. Where the pilgrims imagined it crawled to I don't know. To some place where they expected to get something, I bet! For me it crawled towards Kurtz—exclusively; but when the steam pipes started leaking we crawled very slow. The reaches opened before us and closed behind, as if the forest had stepped leisurely across the water to bar the way for our return. We penetrated deeper and deeper into the heart of darkness. It was very quiet there. At night sometimes the roll of drums behind the curtain of trees would run up the river and remain sustained faintly, as if hovering in the air high over our heads, till the first break of day. Whether it meant war, peace, or prayer we could not tell. The dawns were heralded by the descent of a chill stillness; the woodcutters slept, their fires burned low; the snapping of a twig would make you start. We were wanderers on prehistoric earth, on an earth that wore the aspect

of an unknown planet. We could have fancied ourselves the first of men
taking possession of an accursed inheritance, to be subdued at the cost of
profound anguish and of excessive toil. But suddenly, as we struggled
round a bend, there would be a glimpse of rush walls, of peaked grass
roofs, a burst of yells, a whirl of black limbs, a mass of hands clapping, of
feet stamping, of bodies swaying, of eyes rolling, under the droop of heavy
and motionless foliage. The steamer toiled along slowly on the edge of a
black and incomprehensible frenzy. The prehistoric man was cursing us,
praying to us, welcoming us—who could tell? We were cut off from the
comprehension of our surroundings; we glided past like phantoms, won-
dering and secretly appalled, as sane men would be before an enthusiastic
outbreak in a madhouse. We could not understand because we were too far
and could not remember, because we were traveling in the night of first
ages, of those ages that are gone, leaving hardly a sign—and no memories.

"The earth seemed unearthly. We are accustomed to look upon the
shackled form of a conquered monster, but there—there you could look at
a thing monstrous and free. It was unearthly, and the men were— No, they
were not inhuman. Well, you know, that was the worst of it—this suspicion
of their not being inhuman. It would come slowly to one. They howled and
leaped, and spun, and made horrid faces; but what thrilled you was just
the thought of their humanity—like yours—the thought of your remote
kinship with this wild and passionate uproar. Ugly. Yes, it was ugly
enough; but if you were man enough you would admit to yourself that there
was in you just the faintest trace of a response to the terrible frankness of
that noise, a dim suspicion of there being a meaning in it which you—you
so remote from the night of first ages—could comprehend. And why not?
The mind of man is capable of anything—because everything is in it, all
the past as well as all the future. What was there after all? Joy, fear, sorrow,
devotion, valor, rage—who can tell?—but truth—truth stripped of its
cloak of time. Let the fool gape and shudder—the man knows, and can
look on without a wink. But he must at least be as much of a man as these
on the shore. He must meet that truth with his own true stuff—with his
own inborn strength. Principles won't do. Acquisitions, clothes, pretty
rags—rags that would fly off at the first good shake. No; you want a
deliberate belief. An appeal to me in this fiendish row—is there? Very
well; I hear; I admit, but I have a voice, too, and for good or evil mine is the
speech that cannot be silenced. Of course, a fool, what with sheer fright
and fine sentiments, is always safe. Who's that grunting? You wonder I
didn't go ashore for a howl and a dance? Well, no—I didn't. Fine sentiments, you say? Fine sentiments, be hanged! I had no time. I had to mess
about with white lead and strips of woolen blanket helping to put bandages

on those leaky steam pipes—I tell you. I had to watch the steering, and circumvent those snags, and get the tin-pot along by hook or by crook. There was surface truth enough in these things to save a wiser man. And between whiles I had to look after the savage who was fireman. He was an improved specimen; he could fire up a vertical boiler. He was there below me, and, upon my word, to look at him was as edifying as seeing a dog in a parody of breeches and a feather hat, walking on his hind legs. A few months of training had done for that really fine chap. He squinted at the steam gauge and at the water gauge with an evident effort of intrepidity—and he had filed teeth, too, the poor devil, and the wool of his pate shaved into queer patterns, and three ornamental scars on each of his cheeks. He ought to have been clapping his hands and stamping his feet on the bank, instead of which he was hard at work, a thrall to strange witchcraft, full of improving knowledge. He was useful because he had been instructed; and what he knew was this—that should the water in that transparent thing disappear, the evil spirit inside the boiler would get angry through the greatness of his thirst, and take a terrible vengeance. So he sweated and fired up and watched the glass fearfully (with an impromptu charm, made of rags, tied to his arm, and a piece of polished bone, as big as a watch, stuck flatways through his lower lip), while the wooded banks slipped past us slowly, the short noise was left behind, the interminable miles of silence—and we crept on, towards Kurtz. But the snags were thick, the water was treacherous and shallow, the boiler seemed indeed to have a sulky devil in it, and thus neither that fireman nor I had any time to peer into our creepy thoughts.

"Some fifty miles below the Inner Station we came upon a hut of reeds, an inclined and melancholy pole, with the unrecognizable tatters of what had been a flag of some sort flying from it, and a neatly stacked wood pile. This was unexpected. We came to the bank, and on the stack of firewood found a flat piece of board with some faded pencil writing on it. When deciphered it said: 'Wood for you. Hurry up. Approach cautiously.' There was a signature, but it was illegible—not Kurtz—a much longer word. Hurry up. Where? Up the river? 'Approach cautiously.' We had not done so. But the warning could not have been meant for the place where it could be only found after approach. Something was wrong above. But what—and how much? That was the question. We commented adversely upon the imbecility of that telegraphic style. The bush around said nothing, and would not let us look very far, either. A torn curtain of red twill hung in the doorway of the hut, and flapped sadly in our faces. The dwelling was dismantled; but we could see a white man had lived there not very long ago. There remained a rude table—a plank on two posts; a heap of rubbish reposed in a dark corner, and by the door I picked up a book. It had lost its covers, and the pages had been thumbed into a state of extremely dirty softness; but the back had been lovingly stitched afresh with white cotton thread, which looked clean yet. It was an extraordinary find. Its title was, *An Inquiry into Some Points of Seamanship,* by a man Tower, Towson— some such name—Master in his Majesty's Navy. The matter looked dreary reading enough, with illustrative diagrams and repulsive tables of figures, and the copy was sixty years old. I handled this amazing antiquity with the greatest possible tenderness, lest it should dissolve in my hands. Within, Towson or Towser was inquiring earnestly into the breaking strain of ships' chains and tackle, and other such matters. Not a very enthralling book; but at the first glance you could see there a singleness of intention, an honest concern for the right way of going to work, which made these humble pages, thought out so many years ago, luminous with another than a professional light. The simple old sailor, with his talk of chains and purchases, made me forget the jungle and the pilgrims in a delicious sensation of having come upon something unmistakably real. Such a book being there was wonderful enough; but still more astounding were the notes penciled in the margin, and plainly referring to the text. I couldn't believe my eyes! They were in cipher! Yes, it looked like cipher. Fancy a man lugging with him a book of that description into this nowhere and studying it—and making notes—in cipher at that! It was an extravagant mystery.

"I had been dimly aware for some time of a worrying noise, and when I lifted my eyes I saw the wood pile was gone, and the manager, aided by all the pilgrims, was shouting at me from the river side. I slipped the book into my pocket. I assure you to leave off reading was like tearing myself away from the shelter of an old and solid friendship.

"I started the lame engine ahead. 'It must be this miserable trader— this intruder,' exclaimed the manager, looking back malevolently at the place we had left. 'He must be English,' I said. 'It will not save him from getting into trouble if he is not careful,' muttered the manager darkly. I observed with assumed innocence that no man was safe from trouble in this world.

"The current was more rapid now, the steamer seemed at her last gasp, the stern wheel flopped languidly, and I caught myself listening on tiptoe for the next beat of the boat, for in sober truth I expected the wretched thing to give up every moment. It was like watching the last flickers of a life. But still we crawled. Sometimes I would pick out a tree a little way ahead to measure our progress towards Kurtz by, but I lost it invariably before we got abreast. To keep the eyes so long on one thing was too much for human patience. The manager displayed a beautiful resignation. I fretted and fumed and took to arguing with myself whether or no I would talk openly with Kurtz; but before I could come to any conclusion it occurred to me that my speech or my silence, indeed any action of mine, would be a mere futility. What did it matter what anyone knew or ignored? What did it matter who was manager? One gets sometimes such a flash of insight. The essentials of this affair lay deep under the surface, beyond my reach, and beyond my power of meddling.

"Towards the evening of the second day we judged ourselves about eight miles from Kurtz's station. I wanted to push on; but the manager looked grave, and told me the navigation up there was so dangerous that it would be advisable, the sun being very low already, to wait where we were till next morning. Moreover, he pointed out that if the warning to approach cautiously were to be followed, we must approach in daylight—not at dusk, or in the dark. This was sensible enough. Eight miles meant nearly three hours' steaming for us, and I could also see suspicious ripples at the upper end of the reach. Nevertheless, I was annoyed beyond expression at the delay, and most unreasonably, too, since one night more could not matter much after so many months. As we had plenty of wood, and caution was the word, I brought up in the middle of the stream. The reach was narrow, straight, with high sides like a railway cutting. The dusk came gliding into it long before the sun had set. The current ran smooth and swift, but a dumb immobility sat on the banks. The living trees, lashed together by the creepers and every living bush of the undergrowth, might have been changed into stone, even to the slenderest twig, to the lightest leaf. It was not sleep—it seemed unnatural, like a state of trance. Not the faintest sound of any kind could be heard. You looked on amazed, and began to suspect yourself of being deaf—then the night came suddenly, and struck you blind as well. About three in the morning some large fish leaped, and the loud splash made me jump as though a gun had been fired. When the sun rose there was a white fog, very warm and clammy, and more blinding than the night. It did not shift or drive; it was just there, standing all round you like something solid. At eight or nine, perhaps, it lifted as a shutter lifts. We had a glimpse of the towering multitude of trees, of the immense matted jungle, with the blazing little ball of the sun hanging over it—all perfectly still—and then the white shutter came down again, smoothly, as if sliding in greased grooves. I ordered the chain, which we had begun to heave in, to be paid out again. Before it stopped running with a muffled rattle, a cry, a very loud cry, as of infinite desolation, soared slowly in the opaque air. It ceased. A complaining clamor, modulated in savage discords, filled our ears. The sheer unexpectedness of it made my hair stir under my cap. I don't know how it struck the others: to me it seemed as though the mist itself had screamed, so suddenly, and apparently from all sides at once, did this tumultuous and mournful uproar arise. It culminated in a hurried outbreak of almost intolerably excessive shrieking, which stopped short, leaving us stiffened in a variety of silly attitudes, and obstinately listening to the nearly as appalling and excessive silence. 'Good God! What is the meaning—' stammered at my elbow one of the pilgrims, a little fat man, with sandy hair and red whiskers, who wore sidespring boots, and pink pajamas tucked into his socks. Two others remained openmouthed a whole minute, then dashed into the little cabin, to rush out incontinently and stand darting scared glances, with Winchesters at 'ready' in their hands. What we could see was just the steamer we were on, her outlines blurred as though she had been on the point of dissolving, and a misty strip of water, perhaps two feet broad, around her—and that was all. The rest of the world was nowhere, as far as our eyes and ears were concerned. Just nowhere. Gone, disappeared; swept off without leaving a whisper or a shadow behind.

"I went forward, and ordered the chain to be hauled in short, so as to be ready to trip the anchor and move the steamboat at once if necessary. 'Will they attack?' whispered an awed voice. 'We will be all butchered in this fog,' murmured another. The faces twitched with the strain, the hands trembled slightly, the eyes forgot to wink. It was very curious to see the contrast of expressions of the white men and of the black fellows of our crew, who were as much strangers to that part of the river as we, though their homes were only eight hundred miles away. The whites, of course greatly discomposed, had besides a curious look of being painfully shocked by such an outrageous row. The others had an alert, naturally interested expression; but their faces were essentially quiet, even those of the one or two who grinned as they hauled at the chain. Several exchanged short, grunting phrases, which seemed to settle the matter to their satisfaction. Their headman, a young, broadchested black, severely draped in dark-blue fringed cloths, with fierce nostrils and his hair all done up artfully in oily ringlets, stood near me. 'Aha!' I said, just for good fellowship's sake. 'Catch 'im,' he snapped, with a bloodshot widening of his eyes and a flash of sharp teeth—'catch 'im. Give 'im to us.' 'To you, eh?' I asked; 'what would you do with them?' 'Eat 'im!' he said, curtly, and, leaning his elbow on the rail, looked out into the fog in a dignified and profoundly pensive attitude. I would no doubt have been properly horrified, had it not occurred to me that he and his chaps must be very hungry: that they must have been growing increasingly hungry for at least this month past. They had been engaged for six months (I don't think a single one of them had any clear idea of time, as we at the end of countless ages have. They still belonged to the beginnings of time—had no inherited experience to teach them as it were), and of course, as long as there was a piece of paper written over in accordance with some farcical law or other made down the river, it didn't enter anybody's head to trouble how they would live. Certainly they had brought with them some rotten hippo meat, which couldn't have lasted very long, anyway, even if the pilgrims hadn't, in the midst of a shocking hullabaloo, thrown a considerable quantity of it overboard. It looked like a high-handed proceeding; but it was really a case of legitimate self-defense. You can't breathe dead hippo waking, sleeping, and eating, and at the same time keep your precarious grip on existence. Besides that, they had given them every week three pieces of brass wire, each about nine inches long; and the theory was they were to buy their provisions with that currency in river-side villages. You can see how *that* worked. There were either no villages, or the people were hostile, or the director, who like the rest of us fed out of tins, with an occasional old he-goat thrown in, didn't want to stop the steamer for some more or less recondite reasons. So, unless they swallowed the wire itself, or made loops of it to snare the fishes with, I don't see what good their extravagant salary could be to them. I must say it was paid with a regularity worthy of a large and honorable trading company. For the rest, the only thing to eat— though it didn't look eatable in the least—I saw in their possession was a few lumps of some stuff like half-cooked dough, of a dirty lavender color, they kept wrapped in leaves, and now and then swallowed a piece of, but so small that it seemed done more for the looks of the thing than for any serious purpose of sustenance. Why in the name of all the gnawing devils of hunger they didn't go for us—they were thirty to five—and have a good tuck in for once, amazes me now when I think of it. They were big powerful men, with not much capacity to weigh the consequences, with courage, with strength, even yet, though their skins were no longer glossy and their muscles no longer hard. And I saw that something restraining, one of those human secrets that baffle probability, had come into play there. I looked at them with a swift quickening of interest—not because it occurred to me I might be eaten by them before very long, though I own to you that just then I perceived—in a new light, as it were—how unwholesome the pilgrims looked, and I hoped, yes, I positively hoped, that my aspect was not so— what shall I say?—so—unappetizing: a touch of fantastic vanity which fitted well with the dream-sensation that pervaded all my days at that time. Perhaps I had a little fever, too. One can't live with one's finger everlastingly on one's pulse. I had often 'a little fever,' or a little touch of other things—the playful paw-strokes of the wilderness, the preliminary trifling before the more serious onslaught which came in due course. Yes; I looked at them as you would on any human being, with a curiosity of their impulses, motives, capacities, weaknesses, when brought to the test of an inexorable physical necessity. Restraint! What possible restraint? Was it superstition, disgust, patience, fear—or some kind of primitive honor? No fear can stand up to hunger, no patience can wear it out, disgust simply does not exist where hunger is; and as to superstition, beliefs, and what you may call principles, they are less than chaff in a breeze. Don't you know the devilry of lingering starvation, its exasperating torment, its black thoughts, its somber and brooding ferocity? Well, I do. It takes a man all his inborn strength to fight hunger properly. It's really easier to face bereavement, dishonor, and the perdition of one's soul—than this kind of prolonged hunger. Sad, but true. And these chaps, too, had no earthly reason for any kind of scruple. Restraint! I would just as soon have expected restraint from a hyena prowling amongst the corpses of a battlefield. But there was the fact facing me—the fact dazzling, to be seen, like the foam on the depths of the sea, like a ripple on an unfathomable enigma, a mystery greater—when I thought of it—than the curious, inexplicable note of desperate grief in this savage clamor that had swept by us on the river bank, behind the blind whiteness of the fog.

"Two pilgrims were quarreling in hurried whispers as to which bank. 'Left.' 'No, no; how can you? Right, right, of course.' 'It is very serious,' said the manager's voice behind me; 'I would be desolated if anything should happen to Mr. Kurtz before we came up.' I looked at him, and had not the slightest doubt he was sincere. He was just the kind of man who would wish to preserve appearances. That was his restraint. But when he muttered something about going on at once, I did not even take the trouble to answer him. I knew, and he knew, that it was impossible. Were we to let go our hold of the bottom, we would be absolutely in the air—in space. We wouldn't be able to tell where we were going to—whether up- or downstream, or across—till we fetched against one bank or the other, and then we wouldn't know at first which it was. Of course I made no move. I had no mind for a smashup. You couldn't imagine a more deadly place for a shipwreck. Whether drowned at once or not, we were sure to perish speedily in one way or another. 'I authorize you to take all the risks,' he said, after a short silence. 'I refuse to take any,' I said, shortly; which was just the answer he expected, though its tone might have surprised him. 'Well, I must defer to your judgment. You are captain,' he said, with marked civility. I turned my shoulder to him in sign of my appreciation, and looked into the fog. How long would it last? It was the most hopeless lookout. The approach to this Kurtz grubbing for ivory in the wretched bush was beset by as many dangers as though he had been an enchanted princess sleeping in a fabulous castle. 'Will they attack, do you think?' asked the manager, in a confidential tone.

"I did not think they would attack, for several obvious reasons. The thick fog was one. If they left the bank in their canoes they would get lost in it, as we would be if we attempted to move. Still, I had also judged the jungle of both banks quite impenetrable—and yet eyes were in it, eyes that had seen us. The riverside bushes were certainly very thick; but the undergrowth behind was evidently penetrable. However, during the short lift I had seen no canoes anywhere in the reach—certainly not abreast of the steamer. But what made the idea of attack inconceivable to me was the nature of the noise—of the cries we had heard. They had not the fierce character boding of immediate hostile intention. Unexpected, wild, and violent as they had been, they had given me an irresistible impression of sorrow. The glimpse of the steamboat had for some reason filled those savages with unrestrained grief. The danger, if any, I expounded, was from our proximity to a great human passion let loose. Even extreme grief may ultimately vent itself in violence—but more generally takes the form of apathy. . . .

"You should have seen the pilgrims stare! They had no heart to grin, or even to revile me: but I believe they thought me gone mad—with fright, maybe. I delivered a regular lecture. My dear boys, it was no good bothering. Keep a lookout? Well, you may guess I watched the fog for the signs of lifting as a cat watches a mouse; but for anything else our eyes were of no more use to us than if we had been buried miles deep in a heap of cotton-wool. It felt like it, too—choking, warm, stifling. Besides, all I said, though it sounded extravagant, was absolutely true to fact. What we afterwards alluded to as an attack was really an attempt at repulse. The action was very far from being aggressive—it was not even defensive, in the usual sense: it was undertaken under the stress of desperation, and in its essence was purely protective.

"It developed itself, I should say, two hours after the fog lifted, and its commencement was at a spot, roughly speaking, about a mile and a half below Kurtz's station. We had just floundered and flopped round a bend, when I saw an islet, a mere grassy hummock of bright green, in the middle of the stream. It was the only thing of the kind; but as we opened the reach more, I perceived it was the head of a long sandbank, or rather of a chain of shallow patches stretching down the middle of the river. They were discolored, just awash, and the whole lot was seen just under the water, exactly as a man's backbone is seen running down the middle of his back under the skin. Now, as far as I did see, I could go to the right or to the left of this. I didn't know either channel, of course. The banks looked pretty well alike, the depth appeared the same; but as I had been informed the station was on the west side, I naturally headed for the western passage.

"No sooner had we fairly entered it than I became aware it was much narrower than I had supposed. To the left of us there was the long uninterrupted shoal, and to the right a high, steep bank heavily overgrown with bushes. Above the bush the trees stood in serried ranks. The twigs overhung the current thickly, and from distance to distance a large limb of some tree projected rigidly over the stream. It was then well on in the afternoon, the face of the forest was gloomy, and a broad strip of shadow had already fallen on the water. In this shadow we steamed up—very slowly, as you may imagine. I sheered her well inshore—the water being deepest near the bank, as the sounding pole informed me.

"One of my hungry and forbearing friends was sounding in the bows just below me. This steamboat was exactly like a decked scow. On the deck, there were two little teakwood houses, with doors and windows. The boiler was in the fore-end, and the machinery right astern. Over the whole there was a light roof, supported on stanchions. The funnel projected through that roof, and in front of the funnel a small cabin built of light planks served for a pilot house. It contained a couch, two campstools, a loaded Martini-Henry leaning in one corner, a tiny table, and the steering wheel. It had a wide door in front and a broad shutter at each side. All these were always thrown open, of course. I spent my days perched up there on the extreme fore-end of that roof, before the door. At night I slept, or tried to, on the couch. An athletic black belonging to some coast tribe, and educated by my poor predecessor, was the helmsman. He sported a pair of brass earrings, wore a blue cloth wrapper from the waist to the ankles, and thought all the world of himself. He was the most unstable kind of fool I had ever seen. He steered with no end of a swagger while you were by; but if he lost sight of you, he became instantly the prey of an abject funk, and would let that cripple of a steamboat get the upper hand of him in a minute.

"I was looking down at the sounding pole, and feeling much annoyed to see at each try a little more of it stick out of that river, when I saw my poleman give up the business suddenly, and stretch himself flat on the deck, without even taking the trouble to haul his pole in. He kept hold on it though, and it trailed in the water. At the same time the fireman, whom I could also see below me, sat down abruptly before his furnace and ducked his head. I was amazed. Then I had to look at the river mighty quick, because there was a snag in the fairway. Sticks, little sticks, were flying about—thick: they were whizzing before my nose, dropping below me, striking behind me against my pilot house. All this time the river, the shore, the woods, were very quiet—perfectly quiet. I could only hear the heavy splashing thump of the stern wheel and the patter of these things. We cleared the snag clumsily. Arrows, by Jove! We were being shot at! I stepped in quickly to close the shutter on the land side. That fool helmsman, his hands on the spokes, was lifting his knees high, stamping his feet, champing his mouth, like a reined-in horse. Confound him! And we were staggering within ten feet of the bank. I had to lean right out to swing the heavy shutter, and I saw a face amongst the leaves on the level with my own, looking at me very fierce and steady; and then suddenly, as though a veil had been removed from my eyes, I made out, deep in the tangled gloom, naked breasts, arms, legs, glaring eyes—the bush was swarming with human limbs in movement, glistening, of bronze color. The twigs shook, swayed, and rustled, the arrows flew out of them, and then the shutter came to. 'Steer her straight,' I said to the helmsman. He held his head rigid, face forward; but his eyes rolled, he kept on, lifting and setting down his feet gently, his mouth foamed a little. 'Keep quiet!' I said in a fury. I might just as well have ordered a tree not to sway in the wind. I darted out. Below me there was a great scuffle of feet on the iron deck; confused exclamations; a voice screamed, 'Can you turn back?' I caught sight of a V-shaped ripple on the water ahead. What? Another snag! A fusillade burst out under my feet. The pilgrims had opened with their Winchesters, and were simply squirting lead into that bush. A deuce of a lot of smoke came up and drove slowly forward. I swore at it. Now I couldn't see the ripple or the snag either. I stood in the doorway, peering, and the arrows came in swarms. They might have been poisoned, but they looked as though they wouldn't kill a cat. The bush began to howl. Our woodcutters raised a warlike whoop; the report of a rifle just at my back deafened me. I glanced over my shoulder, and the pilot house was yet full of noise and smoke when I made a dash at the wheel. The fool nigger had dropped everything, to throw the shutter open and let off that Martini-Henry. He stood before the wide opening, glaring, and I yelled at him to come back, while I straightened the sudden twist out of that steamboat. There was no room to turn even if I had wanted to, the snag was somewhere very near ahead in that confounded smoke, there was no time to lose, so I just crowded her into the bank—right into the bank, where I knew the water was deep.

"We tore slowly along the overhanging bushes in a whirl of broken twigs and flying leaves. The fusillade below stopped short, as I had foreseen it would when the squirts got empty. I threw my head back to a glinting whizz that traversed the pilot house, in at one shutter-hole and out at the other. Looking past that mad helmsman, who was shaking the empty rifle and yelling at the shore, I saw vague forms of men running bent double, leaping, gliding, distinct, incomplete, evanescent. Something big appeared in the air before the shutter, the rifle went overboard, and the man stepped back swiftly, looked at me over his shoulder in an extraordinary, profound, familiar manner, and fell upon my feet. The side of his head hit the wheel twice, and the end of what appeared a long cane clattered round and knocked over a little campstool. It looked as though after wrenching that thing from somebody ashore he had lost his balance in the effort. The thin smoke had blown away, we were clear of the snag, and looking ahead I could see that in another hundred yards or so I would be free to sheer off, away from the bank; but my feet felt so very warm and wet that I had to look down. The man had rolled on his back and stared straight up at me; both his hands clutched that cane. It was the shaft of a spear that, either thrown or lunged through the opening, had caught him in the side just below the ribs; the blade had gone in out of sight, after making a frightful gash; my shoes were full; a pool of blood lay very still, gleaming dark-red under the wheel; his eyes shone with an amazing luster. The fusillade burst out again. He looked at me anxiously, gripping the spear like something precious, with an air of being afraid I would try to take it away from him. I had to make an effort to free my eyes from his gaze and attend to the steering. With one hand I felt above my head for the line of the steam whistle, and jerked out screech after screech hurriedly. The tumult of angry and warlike yells was checked instantly, and then from the depths of the woods went out such a tremulous and prolonged wail of mournful fear and utter despair as may be imagined to follow the flight of the last hope from the earth. There was a great commotion in the bush; the shower of arrows stopped, a few dropping shots rang out sharply—then silence, in which the languid beat of the stern wheel came plainly to my ears. I put the helm hard a-starboard at the moment when the pilgrim in pink pajamas, very hot and agitated, appeared in the doorway. 'The manager sends me—' he began in an official tone, and stopped short. 'Good God!' he said, glaring at the wounded man.

"We two whites stood over him, and his lustrous and inquiring glance enveloped us both. I declare it looked as though he would presently put to us some question in an understandable language; but he died without uttering a sound, without moving a limb, without twitching a muscle. Only in the very last moment, as though in response to some sign we could not see, to some whisper we could not hear, he frowned heavily, and that frown gave to his black death mask an inconceivably somber, brooding, and menacing expression. The luster of inquiring glance faded swiftly into vacant glassiness. 'Can you steer?' I asked the agent eagerly. He looked very dubious; but I made a grab at his arm, and he understood at once I meant him to steer whether or no. To tell you the truth, I was morbidly anxious to change my shoes and socks. 'He is dead,' murmured the fellow, immensely impressed. 'No doubt about it,' said I, tugging like mad at the shoelaces. 'And by the way, I suppose Mr. Kurtz is dead as well by this time.'

"For the moment that was the dominant thought. There was a sense of extreme disappointment, as though I had found out I had been striving after something altogether without a substance. I couldn't have been more disgusted if I had traveled all this way for the sole purpose of talking with

Mr. Kurtz. Talking with . . . I flung one shoe overboard, and became aware that that was exactly what I had been looking forward to—a talk with Kurtz. I made the strange discovery that I had never imagined him as doing, you know, but as discoursing. I didn't say to myself, 'Now I will never see him,' or 'Now I will never shake him by the hand,' but, 'now I will never hear him.' The man presented himself as a voice. Not of course that I did not connect him with some sort of action. Hadn't I been told in all the tones of jealousy and admiration that he had collected, bartered, swindled, or stolen more ivory than all the other agents together? That was not the point. The point was in his being a gifted creature, and that of all his gifts the one that stood out pre-eminently, that carried with it a sense of real presence, was his ability to talk, his words—the gift of expression, the bewildering, the illuminating, the most exalted and the most contemptible, the pulsating stream of light, or the deceitful flow from the heart of an impenetrable darkness.

"The other shoe went flying unto the devil-god of that river. I thought, by Jove! it's all over. We are too late; he has vanished—the gift has vanished, by means of some spear, arrow, or club. I will never hear that chap speak after all, and my sorrow had a startling extravagance of emotion, even such as I had noticed in the howling sorrow of these savages in the bush. I couldn't have felt more of lonely desolation somehow, had I been robbed of a belief or had missed my destiny in life. . . . Why do you sigh in this beastly way, somebody? Absurd? Well, absurd. Good Lord! mustn't a man ever—Here, give me some tobacco.". . .

There was a pause of profound stillness, then a match flared, and Marlow's lean face appeared, worn, hollow, with downward folds and dropped eyelids, with an aspect of concentrated attention; and as he took vigorous draws at his pipe, it seemed to retreat and advance out of the night in the regular flicker of the tiny flame. The match went out.

"Absurd!" he cried. "This is the worst of trying to tell. . . . Here you all are, each moored with two good addresses, like a hulk with two anchors, a butcher round one corner, a policeman round another, excellent appetites, and temperature normal—you hear—normal from year's end to year's end. And you say, Absurd! Absurd be—exploded! Absurd! My dear boys, what can you expect from a man who out of sheer nervousness had just flung overboard a pair of new shoes! Now I think of it, it is amazing I did not shed tears. I am, upon the whole, proud of my fortitude. I was cut to the quick at the idea of having lost the inestimable privilege of listening to the gifted Kurtz. Of course I was wrong. The privilege was waiting for me. Oh, yes, I heard more than enough. And I was right, too. A voice. He was very little more than a voice. And I heard—him—it—this voice—other voices—all of them were so little more than voices—and the memory of that time itself lingers around me, impalpable, like a dying vibration of one immense jabber, silly, atrocious, sordid, savage, or simply mean, without any kind of sense. Voices, voices—even the girl herself—now—"

He was silent for a long time.

"I laid the ghost of his gifts at last with a lie," he began, suddenly. "Girl! What? Did I mention a girl? Oh, she is out of it—completely. They—the women I mean—are out of it—should be out of it. We must help them to stay in that beautiful world of their own, lest ours gets worse. Oh, she had to be out of it. You should have heard the disinterred body of Mr. Kurtz saying, 'My Intended.' You would have perceived directly then how completely she was out of it. And the lofty frontal bone of Mr. Kurtz! They say the hair goes on growing sometimes, but this—ah—specimen, was impressively bald. The wilderness had patted him on the head, and, behold, it was like a ball—an ivory ball; it had caressed him, and—lo!—he had withered; it had taken him, loved him, embraced him, got into his veins, consumed his flesh, and sealed his soul to its own by the inconceivable ceremonies of some devilish initiation. He was its spoiled and pampered favorite. Ivory? I should think so. Heaps of it, stacks of it. The old mud shanty was bursting with it. You would think there was not a single tusk left either above or below the ground in the whole country. 'Mostly fossil,' the manager had remarked, disparagingly. It was no more fossil than I am; but they call it fossil when it is dug up. It appears these niggers do bury the tusks sometimes—but evidently they couldn't bury this parcel deep enough to save the gifted Mr. Kurtz from his fate. We filled the steamboat with it, and had to pile a lot on the deck. Thus he could see and enjoy as long as he could see, because the appreciation of his favor had remained with him to the last. You should have heard him say, 'My ivory.' Oh yes, I heard him. 'My Intended, my ivory, my station, my river, my—' everything belonged to him. It made me hold my breath in expectation of hearing the wilderness burst into a prodigious peal of laughter that would shake the fixed stars in their places. Everything belonged to him—but that was a trifle. The thing was to know what he belonged to, how many powers of darkness claimed him for their own. That was the reflection that made you creepy all over. It was impossible—it was not good for one either—trying to imagine. He had taken a high seat amongst the devils of the land—I mean literally. You can't understand. How could you?—with solid pavement under your feet, surrounded by kind neighbors ready to cheer you or to fall on you, stepping delicately between the butcher and the policeman, in the holy terror of scandal and gallows and lunatic asylums—how can you imagine what particular region of the first ages a man's untrammeled feet may take him into by the way of solitude—utter solitude without a policeman—by the way of silence—utter silence, where no warning voice of a kind neighbor can be heard whispering of public opinion? These little things make all the great difference. When they are gone you must fall back upon your own innate strength, upon your own capacity for faithfulness. Of course you may be too much of a fool to go wrong—too dull even to know you are being assaulted by the powers of darkness. I take it, no fool ever made a bargain for his soul with the devil: the fool is too much of a fool, or the devil too much of a devil—I don't know which. Or you may be such a thunderingly exalted creature as to be altogether deaf and blind to anything but heavenly sights and sounds. Then the earth for you is only a standing place—and whether to be like this is your loss or your gain I won't pretend to say. But most of us are neither one nor the other. The earth for us is a place to live in, where we must put up with sights, with sounds, with smells, too, by Jove!—breathe dead hippo, so to speak, and not be contaminated. And there, don't you see? Your strength comes in, the faith in your ability for the digging of unostentatious holes to bury the stuff in—your power of devotion, not to yourself, but to an obscure, back-breaking business. And that's difficult enough. Mind, I am not trying to excuse or even explain—I am trying to account to myself for—for—Mr. Kurtz—for the shade of Mr. Kurtz. This initiated wraith from the back of Nowhere honored me with its amazing confidence before it vanished altogether. This was because it could speak English to me. The original Kurtz had been educated partly in England, and—as he was good enough to say himself—his sympathies were in the right place. His mother was half-English, his father was half-French. All Europe contributed to the making of Kurtz; and by and by I learned that, most appropriately, the International Society for the Suppression of Savage Customs had intrusted him with the making of a report, for its future guidance. And he had written it, too. I've seen it. I've read it. It was eloquent, vibrating with eloquence, but too high-strung, I think. Seventeen pages of close writing he had found time for! But this must have been before his—let us say—nerves, went wrong, and caused him to preside at certain midnight dances ending with unspeakable rites, which—as far as I reluctantly gathered from what I heard at various times—were offered up to him—do you understand?—to Mr. Kurtz himself. But it was a beautiful piece of writing. The opening paragraph, however, in the light of later information, strikes me now as ominous. He began with the argument that we whites, from the point of development we had arrived at, 'must necessarily appear to them [savages] in the nature of supernatural beings—we approach them with the might as of a deity,' and so on, and so on. 'By the simple exercise of our will we can exert a power for good practically unbounded,' etc., etc. From that point he soared and took me with him. The peroration was magnificent, though difficult to remember, you know. It

gave me the notion of an exotic Immensity ruled by an august Benevo-
lence. It made me tingle with enthusiasm. This was the unbounded power
of eloquence—of words—of burning noble words. There were no practical hints to interrupt the magic current of phrases, unless a kind of note at
the foot of the last page, scrawled evidently much later, in an unsteady
hand, may be regarded as the exposition of a method. It was very simple,
and at the end of that moving appeal to every altruistic sentiment it blazed
at you, luminous and terrifying, like a flash of lightning in a serene sky:
'Exterminate all the brutes!' The curious part was that he had apparently
forgotten all about that valuable postscriptum, because, later on, when he
in a sense came to himself, he repeatedly entreated me to take good care of
'my pamphlet' (he called it), as it was sure to have in the future a good
influence upon his career. I had full information about all these things,
and, besides, as it turned out, I was to have the care of his memory. I've
done enough for it to give me the indisputable right to lay it, if I choose, for
an everlasting rest in the dust bin of progress, amongst all the sweepings
and, figuratively speaking, all the dead cats of civilization. But then, you
see, I can't choose. He won't be forgotten. Whatever he was, he was not
common. He had the power to charm or frighten rudimentary souls into an
aggravated witch dance in his honor; he could also fill the small souls of
the pilgrims with bitter misgivings: he had one devoted friend at least, and
he had conquered one soul in the world that was neither rudimentary nor
tainted with self-seeking. No; I can't forget him, though I am not prepared
to affirm the fellow was exactly worth the life we lost in getting to him. I
missed my late helmsman awfully—I missed him even while his body was
still lying in the pilot house. Perhaps you will think it passing strange this
regret for a savage who was no more account than a grain of sand in a black
Sahara. Well, don't you see, he had done something, he had steered; for
months I had him at my back—a help—an instrument. It was a kind of
partnership. He steered for me—I had to look after him, I worried about
his deficiencies, and thus a subtle bond had been created, of which I only
became aware when it was suddenly broken. And the intimate profundity
of that look he gave me when he received his hurt remains to this day in my
memory—like a claim of distant kinship affirmed in a supreme moment.

"Poor fool! If he had only left that shutter alone. He had no restraint, no
restraint—just like Kurtz—a tree swayed by the wind. As soon as I had
put on a dry pair of slippers, I dragged him out, after first jerking the spear
out of his side, which operation I confess I performed with my eyes shut
tight. His heels leaped together over the little doorstep; his shoulders were
pressed to my breast; I hugged him from behind desperately. Oh! he was
heavy, heavy; heavier than any man on earth, I should imagine. Then
without more ado I tipped him overboard. The current snatched him as

though he had been a wisp of grass, and I saw the body roll over twice before I lost sight of it forever. All the pilgrims and the manager were then congregated on the awning deck about the pilot house, chattering at each other like a flock of excited magpies, and there was a scandalized murmur at my heartless promptitude. What they wanted to keep that body hanging about for I can't guess. Embalm it, maybe. But I had also heard another, and a very ominous, murmur on the deck below. My friends the woodcutters were likewise scandalized, and with a better show of reason—though I admit that the reason itself was quite inadmissible. Oh, quite! I had made up my mind that if my late helmsman was to be eaten, the fishes alone should have him. He had been a very second-rate helmsman while alive, but now he was dead he might have become a first-class temptation, and possibly cause some startling trouble. Besides, I was anxious to take the wheel, the man in pink pajamas showing himself a hopeless duffer at the business.

"This I did directly the simple funeral was over. We were going half-speed, keeping right in the middle of the stream, and I listened to the talk about me. They had given up Kurtz, they had given up the station; Kurtz was dead, and the station had been burnt—and so on—and so on. The red-haired pilgrim was beside himself with the thought that at least this poor Kurtz had been properly avenged. 'Say! We must have made a glorious slaughter of them in the bush. Eh? What do you think? Say?' He positively danced, the bloodthirsty little gingery beggar. And he had nearly fainted when he saw the wounded man! I could not help saying, 'You made a glorious lot of smoke, anyhow.' I had seen, from the way the tops of the bushes rustled and flew, that almost all the shots had gone too high. You can't hit anything unless you take aim and fire from the shoulder; but these chaps fired from the hip with their eyes shut. The retreat, I maintained—and I was right—was caused by the screeching of the steam whistle. Upon this they forgot Kurtz, and began to howl at me with indignant protests.

"The manager stood by the wheel murmuring confidentially about the necessity of getting well away down the river before dark at all events, when I saw in the distance a clearing on the river side and the outlines of some sort of building. 'What's this?' I asked. He clapped his hands in wonder. 'That station!' he cried. I edged in at once, still going half-speed.

"Through my glasses I saw the slope of a hill interspersed with rare trees and perfectly free from undergrowth. A long decaying building on the summit was half buried in the high grass; the large holes in the peaked roof gaped black from afar; the jungle and the woods made a background. There was no enclosure or fence of any kind; but there had been one apparently, for near the house half-a-dozen slim posts remained in a row, roughly trimmed, and with their upper ends ornamented with round carved balls. The rails, or whatever there had been between, had disappeared. Of course the forest surrounded all that. The river bank was clear, and on the water side I saw a white man under a hat like a cart wheel beckoning persistently with his whole arm. Examining the edge of the forest above and below, I was almost certain I could see movements—human forms gliding here and there. I steamed past prudently, then stopped the engines and let her drift down. The man on the shore began to shout, urging us to land. 'We have been attacked,' screamed the manager. 'I know—I know. It's all right,' yelled back the other, as cheerful as you please. 'Come along. It's all right. I am glad.'

"His aspect reminded me of something I had seen—something funny I had seen somewhere. As I maneuvered to get alongside, I was asking myself, 'What does this fellow look like?' Suddenly I got it. He looked like a harlequin. His clothes had been made of some stuff that was brown holland probably, but it was covered with patches all over, with bright patches, blue, red, and yellow—patches on the back, patches on the front, patches on elbows, on knees; colored binding around his jacket, scarlet edging at the bottom of his trousers; and the sunshine made him look extremely gay and wonderfully neat withal, because you could see how beautifully all this patching had been done. A beardless, boyish face, very fair, no features to speak of, nose peeling, little blue eyes, smiles and frowns chasing each other over that open countenance like sunshine and shadow on a wind-swept plain. 'Look out, captain!' he cried; 'there's a snag lodged in here last night.' What! Another snag? I confess I swore shamefully. I had nearly holed my cripple, to finish off that charming trip. The harlequin on the bank turned his little pug nose up to me. 'You English?' he asked, all smiles. 'Are you?' I shouted from the wheel. The smiles vanished, and he shook his head as if sorry for my disappointment. Then he brightened up. 'Never mind!' he cried, encouragingly. 'Are we in time?' I asked. 'He is up there,' he replied, with a toss of the head up the hill, and becoming gloomy all of a sudden. His face was like the autumn sky, overcast one moment and bright the next.

"When the manager, escorted by the pilgrims, all of them armed to the teeth, had gone to the house this chap came on board. 'I say, I don't like this. These natives are in the bush,' I said. He assured me earnestly it was all right. 'They are simple people,' he added; 'well, I am glad you came. It took me all my time to keep them off.' 'But you said it was all right,' I cried. 'Oh, they meant no harm,' he said; and as I stared he corrected himself, 'Not exactly.' Then vivaciously, 'My faith, your pilot house wants a clean-up!' In the next breath he advised me to keep enough steam on the boiler to blow the whistle in case of any trouble. 'One good screech will do more for you than all your rifles. They are simple people,' he repeated. He rattled away at such a rate he quite overwhelmed me. He seemed to be trying to make up for lots of silence, and actually hinted, laughing, that such was the case. 'Don't you talk with Mr. Kurtz?' I said. 'You don't talk with that man—you listen to him,' he exclaimed with severe exaltation. 'But now—' He waved his arm, and in the twinkling of an eye was in the uttermost depths of despondency. In a moment he came up again with a jump, possessed himself of both my hands, shook them continuously, while he gabbled: 'Brother sailor . . . honor . . . pleasure . . . delight . . . introduce myself . . . Russian . . . son of an arch-priest . . . Government of Tambov. . . . What? Tobacco! English tobacco; the excellent English tobacco! Now, that's brotherly. Smoke? Where's a sailor that does not smoke?'

"The pipe soothed him, and gradually I made out he had run away from school, had gone to sea in a Russian ship; ran away again; served some time in English ships; was now reconciled with the arch-priest. He made a point of that. 'But when one is young one must see things, gather experience, ideas; enlarge the mind.' 'Here!' I interrupted. 'You can never tell! Here I met Mr. Kurtz,' he said, youthfully solemn and reproachful. I held my tongue after that. It appears he had persuaded a Dutch trading house on the coast to fit him out with stores and goods, and had started for the interior with a light heart, and no more idea of what would happen to him than a baby. He had been wandering about that river for nearly two years alone, cut off from everybody and everything. 'I am not so young as I look. I am twenty-five,' he said. 'At first old Van Shuyten would tell me to go to the devil,' he narrated with keen enjoyment; 'but I stuck to him, and talked and talked, till at last he got afraid I would talk the hind leg off his favorite dog, so he gave me some cheap things and a few guns, and told me he hoped he would never see my face again. Good old Dutchman, Van Shuyten. I've sent him one small lot of ivory a year ago, so that he can't call me a little thief when I get back. I hope he got it. And for the rest I don't care. I had some wood stacked for you. That was my old house. Did you see?'

"I gave him Towson's book. He made as though he would kiss me, but restrained himself. 'The only book I had left, and I thought I had lost it,' he said, looking at it ecstatically. 'So many accidents happen to a man going about alone, you know. Canoes get upset sometimes—and sometimes you've got to clear out so quick when the people get angry.' He thumbed the pages. 'You made notes in Russian?' I asked. He nodded. 'I thought they were written in cipher,' I said. He laughed, then became serious. 'I had lots of trouble to keep these people off,' he said. 'Did they want to kill you?' I asked. 'Oh, no!' he cried, and checked himself. 'Why did they attack us?' I pursued. He hesitated, then said shamefacedly, 'They don't want him to go.' 'Don't they?' I said, curiously. He nodded a nod full of mystery and wisdom. 'I tell you,' he cried, 'this man has enlarged my mind.' He opened his arms wide, staring at me with his little blue eyes that were perfectly round."

III

"I looked at him, lost in astonishment. There he was before me, in motley, as though he had absconded from a troupe of mimes, enthusiastic, fabulous. His very existence was improbable, inexplicable, and altogether bewildering. He was an insoluble problem. It was inconceivable how he had existed, how he had succeeded in getting so far, how he had managed to remain—why he did not instantly disappear. 'I went a little farther,' he said, 'then still a little farther—till I had gone so far that I don't know how I'll ever get back. Never mind. Plenty time. I can manage. You take Kurtz away quick—quick—I tell you.' The glamor of youth enveloped his parti-colored rags, his destitution, his loneliness, the essential desolation of his futile wanderings. For months—for years—his life hadn't been worth a day's purchase; and there he was gallantly, thoughtlessly alive, to all appearance indestructible solely by the virtue of his few years and of his unreflecting audacity. I was seduced into something like admiration—like envy. Glamor urged him on, glamor kept him unscathed. He surely wanted nothing from the wilderness but space to breathe in and to push on through. His need was to exist, and to move onwards at the greatest possible risk, and with a maximum of privation. If the absolutely pure, uncalculating, unpractical spirit of adventure had ever ruled a human being, it ruled this bepatched youth. I almost envied him the possession of this modest and clear flame. It seemed to have consumed all thought of self so completely, that even while he was talking to you, you forgot that it was he—the man before your eyes—who had gone through these things. I did not envy him his devotion to Kurtz, though. He had not meditated over it. It came to him, and he accepted it with a sort of eager fatalism. I must say that to me it appeared about the most dangerous thing in every way he had come upon so far.

"They had come together unavoidably, like two ships becalmed near each other, and lay rubbing sides at last. I suppose Kurtz wanted an audience, because on a certain occasion, when encamped in the forest, they had talked all night, or more probably Kurtz had talked. 'We talked of everything,' he said, quite transported at the recollection. 'I forgot there was such a thing as sleep. The night did not seem to last an hour. Everything! Everything! . . . Of love, too.' 'Ah, he talked to you of love!' I said, much amused. 'It isn't what you think,' he cried, almost passionately. 'It was in general. He made me see things—things.'

"He threw his arms up. We were on deck at the time, and the headman of my woodcutters, lounging near by, turned upon him his heavy and glittering eyes. I looked around, and I don't know why, but I assure you that never, never before, did this land, this river, this jungle, the very arch of this blazing sky, appear to me so hopeless and so dark, so impenetrable to human thought, so pitiless to human weakness. 'And, ever since, you have been with him, of course?' I said.

"On the contrary. It appears their intercourse had been very much broken by various causes. He had, as he informed me proudly, managed to nurse Kurtz through two illnesses (he alluded to it as you would to some risky feat), but as a rule Kurtz wandered alone, far in the depths of the forest. 'Very often coming to this station, I had to wait days and days before he would turn up,' he said. 'Ah, it was worth waiting for!—sometimes.' 'What was he doing? Exploring or what?' I asked. 'Oh, yes, of course'; he had discovered lots of villages, a lake, too—he did not know exactly in what direction; it was dangerous to inquire too much—but mostly his expeditions had been for ivory. 'But he had no goods to trade with by that time,' I objected. 'There's a good lot of cartridges left even yet,' he answered, looking away. 'To speak plainly, he raided the country,' I said. He nodded. 'Not alone, surely!' He muttered something about the villages round that lake. 'Kurtz got the tribe to follow him, did he?' I suggested. He fidgeted a little. 'They adored him,' he said. The tone of these words was so extraordinary that I looked at him searchingly. It was curious to see his mingled eagerness and reluctance to speak of Kurtz. The man filled his life, occupied his thoughts, swayed his emotions. 'What can you expect?' he burst out; 'he came to them with thunder and lightning, you know—and they had never seen anything like it—and very terrible. He could be very terrible. You can't judge Mr. Kurtz as you would an ordinary man. No, no, no! Now—just to give you an idea—I don't mind telling you, he wanted to shoot me, too, one day—but I don't judge him.' 'Shoot you!' I cried. 'What for?' 'Well, I had a small lot of ivory the chief of that village near my house gave me. You see I used to shoot game for them. Well, he wanted it, and wouldn't hear reason. He declared he would shoot me unless I gave him the ivory and then cleared out of the country, because he could do so, and had a fancy for it, and there was nothing on earth to prevent him killing whom he jolly well pleased. And it was true, too. I gave him the ivory. What did I care! But I didn't clear out. No, no. I couldn't leave him. I had to be careful, of course, till we got friendly again for a time. He had his second illness then. Afterwards I had to keep out of the way; but I didn't mind. He was living for the most part in those villages on the lake. When he came down to the river, sometimes he would take to me, and sometimes it was better for me to be careful. This man suffered too much. He hated all this, and somehow he couldn't get away. When I had a chance I begged him to try and leave while there was time; I offered to go back with him. And he would say yes, and then he would remain; go off on another ivory hunt; disappear for weeks; forget himself amongst these people—forget himself—you know.' 'Why! he's mad,' I said. He protested indignantly. Mr. Kurtz couldn't be mad. If I had heard him talk, only two days ago, I wouldn't dare hint at such a thing. . . . I had taken up my binoculars while we talked, and was looking at the shore, sweeping the limit of the forest at each side and at the back of the house. The consciousness of there being people in that bush, so silent, so quiet—as silent and quiet as the ruined house on the hill—made me uneasy. There was no sign on the face of nature of this amazing tale that was not so much told as suggested to me in desolate exclamations, completed by shrugs, in interrupted phrases, in hints ending in deep sighs. The woods were unmoved, like a mask— heavy, like the closed door of a prison—they looked with their air of hidden knowledge, of patient expectation, of unapproachable silence. The Russian was explaining to me that it was only lately that Mr. Kurtz had come down to the river, bringing along with him all the fighting men of that lake tribe. He had been absent for several months—getting himself adored, I suppose—and had come down unexpectedly, with the intention to all appearances of making a raid either across the river or downstream. Evidently the appetite for more ivory had got the better of the—what shall I say?—less material aspirations. However he had got much worse suddenly. 'I heard he was lying helpless, and so I came up—took my chance,' said the Russian. 'Oh, he is bad, very bad.' I directed my glass to the house. There were no signs of life, but there was the ruined roof, the long mud wall peeping above the grass, with three little square window holes, no two of the same size; all this brought within reach of my hand, as it were. And then I made a brusque movement, and one of the remaining posts of that vanished fence leaped up in the field of my glass. You remember I told you I had been struck at the distance by certain attempts at ornamentation, rather remarkable in the ruinous aspect of the place. Now I had suddenly a nearer view, and its first result was to make me throw my head back as if before a blow. Then I went carefully from post to post with my glass, and I saw my mistake. These round knobs were not ornamental but symbolic; they were expressive and puzzling, striking and disturbing—food for thought and also for the vultures if there had been any looking down from the sky; but at all events for such ants as were industrious enough to ascend the pole. They would have been even more impressive, those heads on the stakes, if their faces had not been turned to the house. Only one, the first I had made out, was facing my way. I was not so shocked as you may think. The start back I had given was really nothing but a movement of surprise. I had expected to see a knob of wood there, you know. I returned deliberately to the first I had seen—and there it was, black, dried, sunken, with closed eyelids, a head that seemed to sleep at the top of that pole, and, with the shrunken dry lips showing a narrow white line of the teeth, was smiling, too, smiling continuously at some endless and jocose dream of that eternal slumber.

"I am not disclosing any trade secrets. In fact, the manager said afterwards that Mr. Kurtz's methods had ruined the district. I have no opinion on that point, but I want you clearly to understand that there was nothing exactly profitable in these heads being there. They only showed that Mr. Kurtz lacked restraint in the gratification of his various lusts, that there was something wanting in him—some small matter which, when the pressing need arose, could not be found under his magnificent eloquence. Whether he knew of this deficiency himself I can't say. I think the knowledge came to him at last—only at the very last. But the wilderness had found him out early, and had taken on him a terrible vengeance for the fantastic invasion. I think it had whispered to him things about himself which he did not know, things of which he had no conception till he took counsel with this great solitude—and the whisper had proved irresistibly fascinating. It echoed loudly within him because he was hollow at the core. . . . I put down the glass, and the head that had appeared near enough to be spoken to seemed at once to have leaped away from me into inaccessible distance.

"The admirer of Mr. Kurtz was a bit crestfallen. In a hurried, indistinct voice he began to assure me he had not dared to take these—say, symbols—down. He was not afraid of the natives; they would not stir till Mr. Kurtz gave the word. His ascendancy was extraordinary. The camps of these people surrounded the place, and the chiefs came every day to see him. They would crawl . . . 'I don't want to know anything of the ceremonies used when approaching Mr. Kurtz,' I shouted. Curious, this feeling that came over me that such details would be more intolerable than those heads drying on the stakes under Mr. Kurtz's windows. After all, that was only a savage sight, while I seemed at one bound to have been transported into some lightless region of subtle horrors, where pure, uncomplicated savagery was a positive relief, being something that had a right to exist—obviously—in the sunshine. The young man looked at me with surprise. I suppose it did not occur to him that Mr. Kurtz was no idol of mine. He forgot I hadn't heard any of these splendid monologues on, what was it? On love, justice, conduct of life—or whatnot. If it had come to crawling before Mr. Kurtz, he crawled as much as the veriest savage of them all. I had no idea of the conditions, he said: these heads were the heads of rebels. I shocked him excessively by laughing. Rebels! What would be the next definition I was to hear? There had been enemies, criminals, workers—and these were rebels. Those rebellious heads looked very subdued to me on their sticks. 'You don't know how such a life tries a man like Kurtz,' cried Kurtz's last disciple. 'Well, and you?' I said. 'I! I! I am a simple man. I have no great thoughts. I want nothing from anybody. How can you compare me to? . . .' His feelings were too much for speech, and suddenly he broke down. 'I don't understand,' he groaned. 'I've been doing my best to keep him alive, and that's enough. I had no hand in all this. I have no abilities. There hasn't been a drop of medicine or a mouthful of invalid food for months here. He was shamefully abandoned. A man like this, with such ideas. Shamefully! Shamefully! I—I—haven't slept for the last ten nights. . . .'

"His voice lost itself in the calm of the evening. The long shadows of the forest had slipped downhill while we talked, had gone far beyond the ruined hovel, beyond the symbolic row of stakes. All this was in the gloom, while we down there were yet in the sunshine, and the stretch of the river abreast of the clearing glittered in a still and dazzling splendor, with a murky and overshadowed bend above and below. Not a living soul was seen on the shore. The bushes did not rustle.

"Suddenly round the corner of the house a group of men appeared, as though they had come up from the ground. They waded waist-deep in the grass, in a compact body, bearing an improvised stretcher in their midst. Instantly, in the emptiness of the landscape, a cry arose whose shrillness pierced the still air like a sharp arrow flying straight to the very heart of the land; and, as if by enchantment, streams of human beings—of naked human beings—with spears in their hands, with bows, with shields, with wild glances and savage movements, were poured into the clearing by the dark-faced and pensive forest. The bushes shook, the grass swayed for a time, and then everything stood still in attentive immobility.

" 'Now, if he does not say the right thing to them we are all done for,' said the Russian at my elbow. The knot of men with the stretcher had stopped, too, halfway to the steamer, as if petrified. I saw the man on the stretcher sit up, lank and with an uplifted arm, above the shoulders of the bearers. 'Let us hope that the man who can talk so well of love in general will find some particular reason to spare us this time,' I said. I resented bitterly the absurd danger of our situation, as if to be at the mercy of that atrocious phantom had been a dishonoring necessity. I could not hear a sound, but through my glasses I saw the thin arm extended commandingly, the lower jaw moving, the eyes of that apparition shining darkly far in its bony head that nodded with grotesque jerks. Kurtz—Kurtz—that means short in German—don't it? Well, the name was as true as everything else in his life—and death. He looked at least seven feet long. His covering had fallen off, and his body emerged from it pitiful and appalling as from a winding sheet. I could see the cage of his ribs all astir, the bones of his arm waving. It was as though an animated image of death carved out of old ivory had been shaking its hand with menaces at a motionless crowd of men made of dark and glittering bronze. I saw him open his mouth wide— it gave him a weirdly voracious aspect, as though he had wanted to swallow all the air, all the earth, all the men before him. A deep voice reached me faintly. He must have been shouting. He fell back suddenly. The stretcher shook as the bearers staggered forward again, and almost at the same time I noticed that the crowd of savages was vanishing without any perceptible movement of retreat, as if the forest that had ejected these beings so suddenly had drawn them in again as the breath is drawn in a long aspiration.

"Some of the pilgrims behind the stretcher carried his arms—two shotguns, a heavy rifle, and a light revolver carbine—the thunderbolts of that pitiful Jupiter. The manager bent over him murmuring as he walked beside his head. They laid him down in one of the little cabins—just a room for a bedplace and a campstool or two, you know. We had brought his belated correspondence, and a lot of torn envelopes and open letters littered his bed. His hand roamed feebly amongst these papers. I was struck by the fire of his eyes and the composed languor of his expression. It was not so much the exhaustion of disease. He did not seem in pain. This shadow looked satiated and calm, as though for the moment it had had its fill of all the emotions.

"He rustled one of the letters, and looking straight in my face said, 'I am glad.' Somebody had been writing to him about me. These special recommendations were turning up again. The volume of tone he emitted without effort, almost without the trouble of moving his lips, amazed me. A voice! a voice! It was grave, profound, vibrating, while the man did not seem capable of a whisper. However, he had enough strength in him—factitious no doubt—to very nearly make an end of us, as you shall hear directly.

"The manager appeared silently in the doorway; I stepped out at once and he drew the curtain after me. The Russian, eyed curiously by the pilgrims, was staring at the shore. I followed the direction of his glance.

"Dark human shapes could be made out in the distance, flitting indistinctly against the gloomy border of the forest, and near the river two bronze figures, leaning on tall spears, stood in the sunlight under fantastic headdresses of spotted skins, warlike and still in statuesque repose. And from right to left along the lighted shore moved a wild and gorgeous apparition of a woman.

"She walked with measured steps, draped in striped and fringed cloths, treading the earth proudly, with a slight jingle and flash of barbarous ornaments. She carried her head high; her hair was done in the shape of a helmet; she had brass leggings to the knee, brass wire gauntlets to the elbow, a crimson spot on her tawny cheek, innumerable necklaces of glass beads on her neck; bizarre things, charms, gifts of witch men, that hung about her, glittered and trembled at every step. She must have had the value of several elephant tusks upon her. She was savage and superb, wild-eyed and magnificent; there was something ominous and stately in her deliberate progress. And in the hush that had fallen suddenly upon the whole sorrowful land, the immense wilderness, the colossal body of the fecund and mysterious life seemed to look at her, pensive, as though it had been looking at the image of its own tenebrous and passionate soul.

"She came abreast of the steamer, stood still, and faced us. Her long shadow fell to the water's edge. Her face had a tragic and fierce aspect of wild sorrow and of dumb pain mingled with the fear of some struggling, half-shaped resolve. She stood looking at us without a stir, and like the wilderness itself, with an air of brooding over an inscrutable purpose. A whole minute passed, and then she made a step forward. There was a low jingle, a glint of yellow metal, a sway of fringed draperies, and she stopped as if her heart had failed her. The young fellow by my side growled. The pilgrims murmured at my back. She looked at us all as if her life had depended upon the unswerving steadiness of her glance. Suddenly she opened her bared arms and threw them up rigid above her head, as though in an uncontrollable desire to touch the sky, and at the same time the swift shadows darted out on the earth, swept around on the river, gathering the steamer into a shadowy embrace. A formidable silence hung over the scene.

"She turned away slowly, walked on, following the bank, and passed into the bushes to the left. Once only her eyes gleamed back at us in the dusk of the thickets before she disappeared.

" 'If she had offered to come aboard I really think I would have tried to shoot her,' said the man of patches, nervously. 'I had been risking my life every day for the last fortnight to keep her out of the house. She got in one day and kicked up a row about those miserable rags I picked up in the storeroom to mend my clothes with. I wasn't decent. At least it must have been that, for she talked like a fury to Kurtz for an hour, pointing at me now and then. I don't understand the dialect of this tribe. Luckily for me, I fancy Kurtz felt too ill that day to care, or there would have been mischief. I don't understand. . . . No—it's too much for me. Ah, well, it's all over now.'

"At this moment I heard Kurtz's deep voice behind the curtain: 'Save me!—save the ivory, you mean. Don't tell me. Save me! Why, I've had to save you. You are interrupting my plans now. Sick! Sick! Not so sick as you would like to believe. Never mind. I'll carry my ideas out yet—I will return. I'll show you what can be done. You with your little peddling notions—you are interfering with me. I will return. I . . .'

"The manager came out. He did me the honor to take me under the arm and lead me aside. 'He is very low, very low,' he said. He considered it necessary to sigh, but neglected to be consistently sorrowful. 'We have done all we could for him—haven't we? But there is no disguising the fact, Mr. Kurtz has done more harm than good to the Company. He did not see the time was not ripe for vigorous action. Cautiously, cautiously—that's my principle. We must be cautious yet. The district is closed to us for a time. Deplorable! Upon the whole, the trade will suffer. I don't deny there is a remarkable quantity of ivory—mostly fossil. We must save it, at all events—but look how precarious the position is—and why? Because the method is unsound.' 'Do you,' said I, looking at the shore, 'call it "unsound method?"' 'Without doubt,' he exclaimed, hotly. 'Don't you?' . . .

"'No method at all,' I murmured after a while. 'Exactly,' he exulted. 'I anticipated this. Shows a complete want of judgment. It is my duty to point it out in the proper quarter.' 'Oh,' said I, 'that fellow—what's his name?—the brickmaker, will make a readable report for you.' He appeared confounded for a moment. It seemed to me I had never breathed an atmosphere so vile, and I turned mentally to Kurtz for relief—positively for relief. 'Nevertheless I think Mr. Kurtz is a remarkable man,' I said with emphasis. He started, dropped on me a cold heavy glance, said very quietly, 'he *was*,' and turned his back on me. My hour of favor was over; I found myself lumped along with Kurtz as a partisan of methods for which the time was not ripe: I was unsound! Ah! but it was something to have at least a choice of nightmares.

"I had turned to the wilderness really, not to Mr. Kurtz, who, I was ready to admit, was as good as buried. And for a moment it seemed to me as if I also were buried in a vast grave full of unspeakable secrets. I felt an intolerable weight oppressing my breast, the smell of the damp earth, the unseen presence of victorious corruption, the darkness of an impenetrable night. . . . The Russian tapped me on the shoulder. I heard him mumbling and stammering something about 'brother seaman—couldn't conceal—knowledge of matters that would affect Mr. Kurtz's reputation.' I waited. For him evidently Mr. Kurtz was not in his grave; I suspect that for him Mr. Kurtz was one of the immortals. 'Well!' said I at last, 'speak out. As it happens, I am Mr. Kurtz's friend—in a way.'

"He stated with a good deal of formality that had we not been 'of the same profession,' he would have kept the matter to himself without regard to consequences. 'He suspected there was an active ill will towards him on the part of these white men that—' 'You are right,' I said, remembering a certain conversation I had overheard. 'The manager thinks you ought to be hanged.' He showed a concern at this intelligence which amused me at first. 'I had better get out of the way quietly,' he said, earnestly. 'I can do no more for Kurtz now, and they would soon find some excuse. What's to stop them? There's a military post three hundred miles from here.' 'Well, upon my word,' said I, 'perhaps you had better go if you have any friends amongst the savages near by.' 'Plenty,' he said. 'They are simple people— and I want nothing, you know.' He stood biting his lip, then: 'I don't want any harm to happen to these whites here, but of course I was thinking of Mr. Kurtz's reputation—but you are a brother seaman and—' 'All right,' said I, after a time. 'Mr. Kurtz's reputation is safe with me.' I did not know how truly I spoke.

"He informed me, lowering his voice, that it was Kurtz who had ordered the attack to be made on the steamer. 'He hated sometimes the idea of being taken away—and then again . . . But I don't understand these matters. I am a simple man. He thought it would scare you away—that you would give it up, thinking him dead. I could not stop him. Oh, I had an awful time of it this last month.' 'Very well,' I said. 'He is all right now.' 'Ye-e-es,' he muttered, not very convinced apparently. 'Thanks,' said I; 'I shall keep my eyes open.' 'But quiet—eh?' he urged, anxiously. 'It would be awful for his reputation if anybody here—' I promised a complete discretion with great gravity. 'I have a canoe and three black fellows waiting not very far. I am off. Could you give me a few Martini-Henry cartridges?' I could, and did, with proper secrecy. He helped himself, with a wink at me, to a handful of my tobacco. 'Between sailors—you know— good English tobacco.' At the door of the pilot house he turned round—'I say, haven't you a pair of shoes you could spare?' He raised one leg. 'Look.' The soles were tied with knotted strings sandalwise under his bare feet. I rooted out an old pair, at which he looked with admiration before tucking it under his left arm. One of his pockets (bright red) was bulging with cartridges, from the other (dark blue) peeped 'Towson's Inquiry,' etc., etc. He seemed to think himself excellently well equipped for a renewed encounter with the wilderness. 'Ah! I'll never, never meet such a man again. You ought to have heard him recite poetry—his own, too, it was, he told me. Poetry!' He rolled his eyes at the recollection of these delights. 'Oh, he enlarged my mind!' 'Good-by,' said I. He shook hands and vanished in the night. Sometimes I ask myself whether I had ever really seen him—whether it was possible to meet such a phenomenon! . . .

"When I woke up shortly after midnight his warning came to my mind with its hint of danger that seemed, in the starred darkness, real enough to make me get up for the purpose of having a look round. On the hill a big fire burned, illuminating fitfully a crooked corner of the station house. One of the agents with a picket of a few of our blacks, armed for the purpose, was keeping guard over the ivory; but deep within the forest, red gleams that wavered, that seemed to sink and rise from the ground amongst confused columnar shapes of intense blackness, showed the exact position of the camp where Mr. Kurtz's adorers were keeping their uneasy vigil. The monotonous beating of a big drum filled the air with muffled shocks and a lingering vibration. A steady droning sound of many men chanting each to himself some weird incantation came out from the black, flat wall of the woods as the humming of bees comes out of a hive, and had a strange narcotic effect upon my half-awake senses. I believe I dozed off leaning over the rail, till an abrupt burst of yells, an overwhelming outbreak of a pent-up and mysterious frenzy, woke me up in a bewildered wonder. It was cut short all at once, and the low droning went on with an effect of audible and soothing silence. I glanced casually into the little cabin. A light was burning within, but Mr. Kurtz was not there.

"I think I would have raised an outcry if I had believed my eyes. But I didn't believe them at first—the thing seemed so impossible. The fact is I was completely unnerved by a sheer blank fright, pure abstract terror, unconnected with any distinct shape of physical danger. What made this emotion so overpowering was—how shall I define it?—the moral shock I received, as if something altogether monstrous, intolerable to thought and odious to the soul, had been thrust upon me unexpectedly. This lasted of course the merest fraction of a second, and then the usual sense of commonplace, deadly danger, the possibility of a sudden onslaught and massacre, or something of the kind, which I saw impending, was positively welcome and composing. It pacified me, in fact, so much, that I did not raise an alarm.

"There was an agent buttoned up inside an ulster and sleeping on a chair on deck within three feet of me. The yells had not awakened him; he snored very slightly; I left him to his slumbers and leaped ashore. I did not betray Mr. Kurtz—it was ordered I should never betray him—it was written I should be loyal to the nightmare of my choice. I was anxious to deal with this shadow by myself alone—and to this day I don't know why I was so jealous of sharing with anyone the peculiar blackness of that experience.

"As soon as I got on the bank I saw a trail—a broad trail through the grass. I remember the exultation with which I said to myself, 'He can't walk—he is crawling on all fours—I've got him.' The grass was wet with dew. I strode rapidly with clenched fists. I fancy I had some vague notion of falling upon him and giving him a drubbing. I don't know. I had some imbecile thoughts. The knitting old woman with the cat obtruded herself upon my memory as a most improper person to be sitting at the other end of such an affair. I saw a row of pilgrims squirting lead in the air out of Winchesters held to the hip. I thought I would never get back to the steamer, and imagined myself living alone and unarmed in the woods to an advanced age. Such silly things—you know. And I remember I confounded the beat of the drum with the beating of my heart, and was pleased at its calm regularity.

"I kept to the track though—then stopped to listen. The night was very clear; a dark blue space, sparkling with dew and starlight, in which black things stood very still. I thought I could see a kind of motion ahead of me. I was strangely cocksure of everything that night. I actually left the track and ran in a wide semicircle (I truly believe chuckling to myself) so as to get in front of that stir, of that motion I had seen—if indeed I had seen anything. I was circumventing Kurtz as though it had been a boyish game.

"I came upon him, and, if he had not heard me coming, I would have fallen over him, too, but he got up in time. He rose, unsteady, long, pale, indistinct, like a vapor exhaled by the earth, and swayed slightly, misty and silent before me; while at my back the fires loomed between the trees, and the murmur of many voices issued from the forest. I had cut him off cleverly; but when actually confronting him I seemed to come to my senses, I saw the danger in its right proportion. It was by no means over yet. Suppose he began to shout? Though he could hardly stand, there was still plenty of vigor in his voice. 'Go away—hide yourself,' he said, in that profound tone. It was very awful. I glanced back. We were within thirty yards from the nearest fire. A black figure stood up, strode on long black legs, waving long black arms, across the glow. It had horns—antelope horns, I think—on its head. Some sorcerer, some witch man, no doubt: it looked fiend-like enough. 'Do you know what you are doing?' I whispered. 'Perfectly,' he answered, raising his voice for that single word: it sounded to me far off and yet loud, like a hail through a speaking trumpet. If he makes a row we are lost, I thought to myself. This clearly was not a case for fisticuffs, even apart from the very natural aversion I had to beat that Shadow—this wandering and tormented thing. 'You will be lost,' I said— 'utterly lost.' One gets sometimes such a flash of inspiration, you know. I did say the right thing, though indeed he could not have been more irretrievably lost than he was at this very moment, when the foundations of our intimacy were being laid—to endure—to endure—even to the end— even beyond.

" 'I had immense plans,' he muttered irresolutely. 'Yes,' said I; 'but if you try to shout I'll smash your head with—' There was not a stick or a stone near. 'I will throttle you for good,' I corrected myself. 'I was on the threshold of great things,' he pleaded, in a voice of longing, with a wistfulness of tone that made my blood run cold. 'And now for this stupid scoundrel—' 'Your success in Europe is assured in any case,' I affirmed, steadily. I did not want to have the throttling of him, you understand—and indeed it would have been very little use for any practical purpose. I tried to break the spell—the heavy, mute spell of the wilderness—that seemed to draw him to its pitiless breast by the awakening of forgotten and brutal instincts, by the memory of gratified and monstrous passions. This alone, I was convinced, had driven him out to the edge of the forest, to the bush, towards the gleam of fires, the throb of drums, the drone of weird incantations; this alone had beguiled his unlawful soul beyond the bounds of permitted aspirations. And, don't you see, the terror of the position was not in being knocked on the head—though I had a very lively sense of that danger, too—but in this, that I had to deal with a being to whom I could not appeal in the name of anything high or low. I had, even like the niggers, to invoke him—himself—his own exalted and incredible degradation. There was nothing either above or below him, and I knew it. He had kicked himself loose of the earth. Confound the man! he had kicked the very earth to pieces. He was alone, and I before him did not know whether I stood on the ground or floated in the air. I've been telling you what we said—repeating the phrases we pronounced—but what's the good? They were common everyday words—the familiar, vague sounds exchanged on every waking day of life. But what of that? They had behind them, to my mind, the terrific suggestiveness of words heard in dreams, of phrases spoken in nightmares. Soul! If anybody had ever struggled with a soul, I am the man. And I wasn't arguing with a lunatic either. Believe me or not, his intelligence was perfectly clear—concentrated, it is true, upon himself with horrible intensity, yet clear; and therein was my only chance—barring, of course, the killing him there and then, which wasn't so good, on account of unavoidable noise. But his soul was mad. Being alone in the wilderness, it had looked within itself, and, by heavens! I tell you, it had gone mad. I had—for my sins, I suppose—to go through the ordeal of looking into it myself. No eloquence could have been so withering to one's belief in mankind as his final burst of sincerity. He struggled with himself, too. I saw it, I heard it. I saw the inconceivable mystery of a soul that knew no restraint, no faith, and no fear, yet struggling blindly with itself. I kept my head pretty well; but when I had him at last stretched on the couch, I wiped my forehead, while my legs shook under me as though I had carried half a ton on my back down that hill. And yet I had only supported him, his bony arm clasped round my neck—and he was not much heavier than a child.

"When next day we left at noon, the crowd, of whose presence behind the curtain of trees I had been acutely conscious all the time, flowed out of the woods again, filled the clearing, covered the slope with a mass of naked, breathing, quivering, bronze bodies. I steamed up a bit, then swung downstream, and two thousand eyes followed the evolutions of the splashing, thumping, fierce river-demon beating the water with its terrible tail and breathing black smoke into the air. In front of the first rank, along the river, three men, plastered with bright red earth from head to foot, strutted to and fro restlessly. When we came abreast again, they faced the river, stamped their feet, nodded their horned heads, swayed their scarlet bodies; they shook towards the fierce river-demon a bunch of black feathers, a mangy skin with a pendent tail—something that looked like a dried gourd; they shouted periodically together strings of amazing words that resembled no sounds of human language; and the deep murmurs of the crowd, interrupted suddenly, were like the responses of some satanic litany.

"We had carried Kurtz into the pilot house: there was more air there. Lying on the couch, he stared through the open shutter. There was an eddy in the mass of human bodies, and the woman with helmeted head and tawny cheeks rushed out to the very brink of the stream. She put out her hands, shouted something, and all that wild mob took up the shout in a roaring chorus of articulated, rapid, breathless utterance.

" 'Do you understand this?' I asked.

"He kept on looking out past me with fiery, longing eyes, with a mingled expression of wistfulness and hate. He made no answer, but I saw a smile, a smile of indefinable meaning, appear on his colorless lips that a moment after twitched convulsively. 'Do I not?' he said slowly, gasping, as if the words had been torn out of him by a supernatural power.

"I pulled the string of the whistle, and I did this because I saw the pilgrims on deck getting out their rifles with an air of anticipating a jolly lark. At the sudden screech there was a movement of abject terror through that wedged mass of bodies. 'Don't! Don't you frighten them away,' cried someone on deck disconsolately. I pulled the string time after time. They broke and ran, they leaped, they crouched, they swerved, they dodged the flying terror of the sound. The three red chaps had fallen flat, face down on the shore, as though they had been shot dead. Only the barbarous and superb woman did not so much as flinch, and stretched tragically her bare arms after us over the somber and glittering river.

"And then that imbecile crowd down on the deck started their little fun, and I could see nothing more for smoke.

"The brown current ran swiftly out of the heart of darkness, bearing us down towards the sea with twice the speed of our upward progress; and Kurtz's life was running swiftly, too, ebbing, ebbing out of his heart into the sea of inexorable time. The manager was very placid, he had no vital anxieties now, he took us both in with a comprehensive and satisfied glance: the 'affair' had come off as well as could be wished. I saw the time approaching when I would be left alone of the party of 'unsound method.' The pilgrims looked upon me with disfavor. I was, so to speak, numbered with the dead. It is strange how I accepted this unforeseen partnership, this choice of nightmares forced upon me in the tenebrous land invaded by these mean and greedy phantoms.

"Kurtz discoursed. A voice! a voice! It rang deep to the very last. It survived his strength to hide in the magnificent folds of eloquence the barren darkness of his heart. Oh, he struggled! he struggled! The wastes of his weary brain were haunted by shadowy images now—images of wealth and fame revolving obsequiously round his unextinguishable gift of noble and lofty expression. My Intended, my station, my career, my ideas— these were the subjects for the occasional utterances of elevated sentiments. The shade of the original Kurtz frequented the bedside of the hollow sham, whose fate it was to be buried presently in the mold of primeval earth. But both the diabolic love and the unearthly hate of the mysteries it had penetrated fought for the possession of that soul satiated with primitive emotions, avid of lying fame, of sham distinction, of all the appearances of success and power.

"Sometimes he was contemptibly childish. He desired to have kings meet him at railway stations on his return from some ghastly Nowhere, where he intended to accomplish great things. 'You show them you have in you something that is really profitable, and then there will be no limits to the recognition of your ability,' he would say. 'Of course you must take care of the motives—right motives—always.' The long reaches that were like one and the same reach, monotonous bends that were exactly alike, slipped past the steamer with their multitude of secular trees looking patiently after this grimy fragment of another world, the forerunner of change, of conquest, of trade, of massacres, of blessings. I looked ahead—piloting. 'Close the shutter,' said Kurtz suddenly one day; 'I can't bear to look at this.' I did so. There was a silence. 'Oh, but I will wring your heart yet!' he cried at the invisible wilderness.

"We broke down—as I had expected—and had to lie-up for repairs at the head of an island. This delay was the first thing that shook Kurtz's confidence. One morning he gave me a packet of papers and a photograph—the lot tied together with a shoestring. 'Keep this for me,' he said. 'This noxious fool' (meaning the manager) 'is capable of prying into my boxes when I am not looking.' In the afternoon I saw him. He was lying on his back with closed eyes, and I withdrew quietly, but I heard him mutter, 'Live rightly, die, die. . . .' I listened. There was nothing more. Was he rehearsing some speech in his sleep, or was it a fragment of a phrase from some newspaper article? He had been writing for the papers and meant to do so again, 'for the furthering of my ideas. It's a duty.'

"His was an impenetrable darkness. I looked at him as you peer down at a man who is lying at the bottom of a precipice where the sun never shines. But I had not much time to give him, because I was helping the engine driver to take to pieces the leaky cylinders, to straighten a bent connecting rod, and in other such matters. I lived in an infernal mess of rust, filings, nuts, bolts, spanners, hammers, ratchet drills—things I abominate, because I don't get on with them. I tended the little forge we fortunately had aboard; I toiled wearily in a wretched scrapheap—unless I had the shakes too bad to stand.

"One evening coming in with a candle I was startled to hear him say a little tremulously, 'I am lying here in the dark waiting for death.' The light was within a foot of his eyes. I forced myself to murmur, 'Oh, nonsense!' and stood over him as if transfixed.

"Anything approaching the change that came over his features I have never seen before, and hope never to see again. Oh, I wasn't touched. I was fascinated. It was as though a veil had been rent. I saw on that ivory face the expression of somber pride, of ruthless power, of craven terror—of an intense and hopeless despair. Did he live his life again in every detail of desire, temptation, and surrender during that supreme moment of complete knowledge? He cried in a whisper at some image, at some vision—he cried out twice, a cry that was no more than a breath: 'The horror! The horror!'

"I blew the candle out and left the cabin. The pilgrims were dining in the messroom, and I took my place opposite the manager, who lifted his eyes to give me a questioning glance, which I successfully ignored. He leaned back, serene, with that peculiar smile of his sealing the unexpressed depths of his meanness. A continuous shower of small flies streamed upon the lamp, upon the cloth, upon our hands and faces. Suddenly the manager's boy put his insolent black head in the doorway, and said in a tone of scathing contempt—

"'Mistah Kurtz—he dead.'

"All the pilgrims rushed out to see. I remained, and went on with my dinner. I believe I was considered brutally callous. However, I did not eat much. There was a lamp in there—light, don't you know—and outside it was so beastly, beastly dark. I went no more near the remarkable man who had pronounced a judgment upon the adventures of his soul on this earth. The voice was gone. What else had been there? But I am of course aware that next day the pilgrims buried something in a muddy hole.

"And then they very nearly buried me.

"However, as you see, I did not go to join Kurtz there and then. I did not. I remained to dream the nightmare out to the end, and to show my loyalty to Kurtz once more. Destiny. My destiny! Droll thing life is—that mysterious arrangement of merciless logic for a futile purpose. The most you can hope from it is some knowledge of yourself—that comes too late— a crop of unextinguishable regrets. I have wrestled with death. It is the most unexciting contest you can imagine. It takes place in an impalpable grayness, with nothing underfoot, with nothing around, without specta- tors, without clamor, without glory, without the great desire of victory, without the great fear of defeat, in a sickly atmosphere of tepid skepticism, without much belief in your own right, and still less in that of your adversary. If such is the form of ultimate wisdom, then life is a greater riddle than some of us think it to be. I was within a hair's-breadth of the last opportunity for pronouncement, and I found with humiliation that probably I would have nothing to say. This is the reason why I affirm that Kurtz was a remarkable man. He had something to say. He said it. Since I had peeped over the edge myself, I understand better the meaning of his stare, that could not see the flame of the candle, but was wide enough to embrace the whole universe, piercing enough to penetrate all the hearts that beat in the darkness. He had summed up—he had judged. 'The horror!' He was a remarkable man. After all, this was the expression of some sort of belief; it had candor, it had conviction, it had a vibrating note of revolt in its whisper, it had the appalling face of a glimpsed truth—the strange commingling of desire and hate. And it is not my own extremity I remember best—a vision of grayness without form filled with physical pain, and a careless contempt for the evanescence of all things—even of this pain itself. No! It is his extremity that I seem to have lived through. True, he had made that last stride, he had stepped over the edge, while I had been permitted to draw back my hesitating foot. And perhaps in this is the whole difference; perhaps all the wisdom, and all truth, and all sincerity, are just compressed into that inappreciable moment of time in which we step over the threshold of the invisible. Perhaps! I like to think my summing-up would not have been a word of careless contempt. Better his cry—much better. It was an affirmation, a moral victory paid for by innumerable defeats, by abominable terrors, by abominable satisfactions. But it was a victory! That is why I have remained loyal to Kurtz to the last, and even beyond, when a long time after I heard once more, not his own voice, but the echo of his magnificent eloquence thrown to me from a soul as translucently pure as a cliff of crystal.

"No, they did not bury me, though there is a period of time which I remember mistily, with a shuddering wonder, like a passage through some inconceivable world that had no hope in it and no desire. I found myself back in the sepulchral city resenting the sight of people hurrying through the streets to filch a little money from each other, to devour their infamous cookery, to gulp their unwholesome beer, to dream their insignificant and silly dreams. They trespassed upon my thoughts. They were intruders whose knowledge of life was to me an irritating pretense, because I felt so sure they could not possibly know the things I knew. Their bearing, which was simply the bearing of commonplace individuals going about their business in the assurance of perfect safety, was offensive to me like the outrageous flauntings of folly in the face of a danger it is unable to comprehend. I had no particular desire to enlighten them, but I had some difficulty in restraining myself from laughing in their faces, so full of stupid importance. I daresay I was not very well at that time. I tottered about the streets—there were various affairs to settle—grinning bitterly at perfectly respectable persons. I admit my behavior was inexcusable, but then my temperature was seldom normal in these days. My dear aunt's endeavors to 'nurse up my strength' seemed altogether beside the mark. It was not my strength that wanted nursing, it was my imagination that wanted soothing. I kept the bundle of papers given me by Kurtz, not knowing exactly what to do with it. His mother had died lately, watched over, as I was told, by his Intended. A clean-shaved man, with an official manner and wearing gold-rimmed spectacles, called on me one day and made inquiries, at first circuitous, afterwards suavely pressing, about what he was pleased to denominate certain 'documents.' I was not surprised, because I had had two rows with the manager on the subject out there. I had refused to give up the smallest scrap out of that package, and I took the same attitude with the spectacled man. He became darkly menacing at last, and with much heat argued that the company had the right to every bit of information about its 'territories.' And said he, 'Mr. Kurtz's knowledge of unexplored regions must have been necessarily extensive and peculiar—owing to his great abilities and to the deplorable circumstances in which he had been placed: therefore—' I assured him Mr. Kurtz's knowledge, however extensive, did not bear upon the problems of commerce or administration. He invoked then the name of science. 'It would be an incalculable loss if,' etc., etc. I offered him the report on the 'Suppression of Savage Customs,' with the postscriptum torn off. He took it up eagerly, but ended by sniffing at it with an air of contempt. 'This is not what we had a right to expect,' he remarked. 'Expect nothing else,' I said. 'There are only private letters.' He withdrew upon some threat of legal proceedings, and I saw him no more; but another fellow, calling himself Kurtz's cousin, appeared two days later, and was anxious to hear all the details about his dear relative's last moments. Incidentally he gave me to understand that Kurtz had been essentially a great musician. 'There was the making of an immense success,' said the man, who was an organist, I believe, with lank gray hair flowing over a greasy coat collar. I had no reason to doubt his statement; and to this day I am unable to say what was Kurtz's profession, whether he ever had any—which was the greatest of his talents. I had taken him for a painter who wrote for the papers, or else for a journalist who could paint—but even the cousin (who took snuff during the interview) could not tell me what he had been—exactly. He was a universal genius—on that point I agreed with the old chap, who thereupon blew his nose noisily into a large cotton handkerchief and withdrew in senile agitation, bearing off some family letters and memoranda without importance. Ultimately a journalist anxious to know something of the fate of his 'dear colleague' turned up. This visitor informed me Kurtz's proper sphere ought to have been politics 'on the popular side.' He had furry straight eyebrows, bristly hair cropped short, an eyeglass on a broad ribbon, and, becoming expansive, confessed his opinion that Kurtz really couldn't write a bit—'but heavens! how that man could talk. He electrified large meetings. He had faith—don't you see?—he had the faith. He could get himself to believe anything—anything. He would have been a splendid leader of an extreme party.' 'What party?' I asked. 'Any party,' answered the other. 'He was an—an—extremist.' Did I not think so? I assented. Did I know, he asked, with a sudden flash of curiosity, 'what it was that had induced him to go out there?' 'Yes,' said I, and forthwith handed him the famous report for publication, if he thought fit. He glanced through it hurriedly, mumbling all the time, judged 'it would do,' and took himself off with this plunder.

"Thus I was left at last with a slim packet of letters and the girl's portrait. She struck me as beautiful—I mean she had a beautiful expression. I know that the sunlight can be made to lie, too, yet one felt that no manipulation of light and pose could have conveyed the delicate shade of truthfulness upon those features. She seemed ready to listen without mental reservation, without suspicion, without a thought for herself. I concluded I would go and give her back her portrait and those letters myself. Curiosity? Yes; and also some other feeling perhaps. All that had been Kurtz's had passed out of my hands: his soul, his body, his station, his plans, his ivory, his career. There remained only his memory and his Intended—and I wanted to give that up, too, to the past, in a way—to surrender personally all that remained of him with me to that oblivion which is the last word of our common fate. I don't defend myself. I had no clear perception of what it was I really wanted. Perhaps it was an impulse of unconscious loyalty, or the fulfilment of one of these ironic necessities that lurk in the facts of human existence. I don't know. I can't tell. But I went.

"I thought his memory was like the other memories of the dead that

accumulate in every man's life—a vague impress on the brain of shadows
that had fallen on it in their swift and final passage; but before the high and
ponderous door, between the tall houses of a street as still and decorous as
a well-kept alley in a cemetery, I had a vision of him on the stretcher,
opening his mouth voraciously, as if to devour all the earth with all its
mankind. He lived then before me; he lived as much as he had ever
lived—a shadow insatiable of splendid appearances, of frightful realities;
a shadow darker than the shadow of the night, and draped nobly in the
folds of a gorgeous eloquence. The vision seemed to enter the house with
me—the stretcher, the phantom-bearers, the wild crowd of obedient
worshipers, the gloom of the forests, the glitter of the reach between the
murky bends, the beat of the drum, regular and muffled like the beating of
a heart—the heart of a conquering darkness. It was a moment of triumph
for the wilderness, an invading and vengeful rush which, it seemed to me,
I would have to keep back alone for the salvation of another soul. And the
memory of what I had heard him say afar there, with the horned shapes
stirring at my back, in the glow of fires, within the patient woods, those
broken phrases came back to me, were heard again in their ominous and
terrifying simplicity. I remembered his abject pleading, his abject threats,
the colossal scale of his vile desires, the meanness, the torment, the
tempestuous anguish of his soul. And later on I seemed to see his collected
languid manner, when he said one day, 'This lot of ivory now is really
mine. The company did not pay for it. I collected it myself at a very great
personal risk. I am afraid they will try to claim it as theirs though. H'm. It
is a difficult case. What do you think I ought to do—resist? Eh? I want no
more than justice.' . . . He wanted no more than justice—no more than
justice. I rang the bell before a mahogany door on the first floor, and while
I waited he seemed to stare at me out of the glassy panel—stare with that
wide and immense stare embracing, condemning, loathing all the universe. I seemed to hear the whispered cry, 'The horror! The horror!'

"The dusk was falling. I had to wait in a lofty drawing room with three
long windows from floor to ceiling that were like three luminous and
bedraped columns. The bent gilt legs and backs of the furniture shone in
indistinct curves. The tall marble fireplace had a cold and monumental
whiteness. A grand piano stood massively in a corner; with dark gleams on
the flat surfaces like a somber and polished sarcophagus. A high door
opened—closed. I rose.

"She came forward, all in black, with a pale head, floating towards me
in the dusk. She was in mourning. It was more than a year since his death,
more than a year since the news came; she seemed as though she would
remember and mourn forever. She took both my hands in hers and
murmured, 'I had heard you were coming.' I noticed she was not very

young—I mean not girlish. She had a mature capacity for fidelity, for belief, for suffering. The room seemed to have grown darker, as if all the sad light of the cloudy evening had taken refuge on her forehead. This fair hair, this pale visage, this pure brow, seemed surrounded by an ashy halo from which the dark eyes looked out at me. Their glance was guileless, profound, confident, and trustful. She carried her sorrowful head as though she were proud of that sorrow, as though she would say, I—I alone know how to mourn for him as he deserves. But while we were still shaking hands, such a look of awful desolation came upon her face that I perceived she was one of those creatures that are not the playthings of Time. For her he had died only yesterday. And, by Jove! the impression was so powerful that for me, too, he seemed to have died only yesterday—nay, this very minute. I saw her and him in the same instant of time—his death and her sorrow—I saw her sorrow in the very moment of his death. Do you understand? I saw them together—I heard them together. She had said, with a deep catch of the breath, 'I have survived' while my strained ears seemed to hear distinctly, mingled with her tone of despairing regret, the summing-up whisper of his eternal condemnation. I asked myself what I was doing there, with a sensation of panic in my heart as though I had blundered into a place of cruel and absurd mysteries not fit for a human being to behold. She motioned me to a chair. We sat down. I laid the packet gently on the little table, and she put her hand over it. . . . 'You knew him well,' she murmured, after a moment of mourning silence.

" 'Intimacy grows quickly out there,' I said. 'I knew him as well as it is possible for one man to know another.'

" 'And you admired him,' she said. 'It was impossible to know him and not to admire him. Was it?'

" 'He was a remarkable man,' I said, unsteadily. Then before the appealing fixity of her gaze, that seemed to watch for more words on my lips, I went on, 'It was impossible not to—'

" 'Love him,' she finished eagerly, silencing me into an appalled dumbness. 'How true! how true! But when you think that no one knew him so well as I! I had all his noble confidence. I knew him best.'

" 'You knew him best,' I repeated. And perhaps she did. But with every word spoken the room was growing darker, and only her forehead, smooth and white, remained illumined by the unextinguishable light of belief and love.

" 'You were his friend,' she went on. 'His friend,' she repeated, a little louder. 'You must have been, if he had given you this, and sent you to me. I feel I can speak to you—and oh! I must speak. I want you—you who have heard his last words—to know I have been worthy of him. . . . It is not pride. . . . Yes! I am proud to know I understood him better than anyone on earth—he told me so himself. And since his mother died I have had no one—no one—to—to—'

"I listened. The darkness deepened. I was not even sure whether he had given me the right bundle. I rather suspect he wanted me to take care of another batch of his papers which, after his death, I saw the manager examining under the lamp. And the girl talked, easing her pain in the certitude of my sympathy; she talked as thirsty men drink. I had heard that her engagement with Kurtz had been disapproved by her people. He wasn't rich enough or something. And indeed I don't know whether he had not been a pauper all his life. He had given me some reason to infer that it was his impatience of comparative poverty that drove him out there.

" '. . . Who was not his friend who had heard him speak once?' she was saying. 'He drew men towards him by what was best in them.' She looked at me with intensity. 'It is the gift of the great,' she went on, and the sound of her low voice seemed to have the accompaniment of all the other sounds, full of mystery, desolation, and sorrow, I had ever heard—the ripple of the river, the soughing of the trees swayed by the wind, the murmurs of the crowds, the faint ring of incomprehensible words cried from afar, the whisper of a voice speaking from beyond the threshold of an eternal darkness. 'But you have heard him! You know!' she cried.

" 'Yes, I know,' I said with something like despair in my heart, but bowing my head before the faith that was in her, before that great and saving illusion that shone with an unearthly glow in the darkness, in the triumphant darkness from which I could not have defended her—from which I could not even defend myself.

" 'What a loss to me—to us!'—she corrected herself with beautiful generosity; then added in a murmur, 'To the world.' By the last gleams of twilight I could see the glitter of her eyes, full of tears—of tears that would not fall.

" 'I have been very happy—very fortunate—very proud,' she went on. 'Too fortunate. Too happy for a little while. And now I am unhappy for—for life.'

"She stood up; her fair hair seemed to catch all the remaining light in a glimmer of gold. I rose, too.

" 'And of all this,' she went on, mournfully, 'of all his promise, and of all his greatness, of his generous mind, of his noble heart, nothing remains—nothing but a memory. You and I—'

" 'We shall always remember him,' I said, hastily.

" 'No!' she cried. 'It is impossible that all this should be lost—that such a life should be sacrificed to leave nothing—but sorrow. You know what vast plans he had. I knew of them, too—I could not perhaps understand—but others knew of them. Something must remain. His words, at least, have not died.'

" 'His words will remain,' I said.

" 'And his example,' she whispered to herself. 'Men looked up to him—his goodness shone in every act. His example—'

" 'True,' I said; 'his example, too. Yes, his example. I forgot that.'

" 'But I do not. I cannot—I cannot believe—not yet. I cannot believe that I shall never see him again, that nobody will see him again, never, never, never.'

"She put out her arms as if after a retreating figure, stretching them black and with clasped pale hands across the fading and narrow sheen of the window. Never see him! I saw him clearly enough then. I shall see this eloquent phantom as long as I live, and I shall see her, too, a tragic and familiar Shade, resembling in this gesture another one, tragic also, and bedecked with powerless charms, stretching bare brown arms over the glitter of the infernal stream, the stream of darkness. She said suddenly very low, 'He died as he lived.'

" 'His end,' said I, with dull anger stirring in me, 'was in every way worthy of his life.'

" 'And I was not with him,' she murmured. My anger subsided before a feeling of infinite pity.

" 'Everything that could be done—' I mumbled.

" 'Ah, but I believed in him more than anyone on earth—more than his own mother, more than—himself. He needed me! Me! I would have treasured every sigh, every word, every sign, every glance.'

"I felt like a chill grip on my chest. 'Don't,' I said, in a muffled voice.

" 'Forgive me. I—I—have mourned so long in silence—in silence. . . . You were with him—to the last? I think of his loneliness. Nobody near to understand him as I would have understood. Perhaps no one to hear. . . .'

" 'To the very end,' I said, shakily. 'I heard his very last words. . . .' I stopped in a fright.

" 'Repeat them,' she murmured in a heartbroken tone. 'I want—I want—something—something—to—to live with.'

"I was on the point of crying at her, 'Don't you hear them?' The dusk was repeating them in a persistent whisper all around us, in a whisper that seemed to swell menacingly like the first whisper of a rising wind. 'The horror! the horror!'

" 'His last word—to live with,' she insisted. 'Don't you understand I loved him—I loved him—I loved him!'

"I pulled myself together and spoke slowly.

" 'The last word he pronounced was—your name.'

"I heard a light sigh and then my heart stood still, stopped dead short by an exulting and terrible cry, by the cry of inconceivable triumph and of unspeakable pain. 'I knew it—I was sure!' . . . She knew. She was sure. I heard her weeping; she had hidden her face in her hands. It seemed to me that the house would collapse before I could escape, that the heavens would fall upon my head. But nothing happened. The heavens do not fall for such a trifle. Would they have fallen, I wonder, if I had rendered Kurtz that justice which was his due? Hadn't he said he wanted only justice? But I couldn't. I could not tell her. It would have been too dark—too dark altogether. . . ."

Marlow ceased, and sat apart, indistinct and silent, in the pose of a meditating Buddha. Nobody moved for a time. "We have lost the first of the ebb," said the director, suddenly. I raised my head. The offing was barred by a black bank of clouds, and the tranquil waterway leading to the uttermost ends of the earth flowed somber under an overcast sky—seemed to lead into the heart of an immense darkness.

London

Study Guide

Text by
Frank Fiorenza
(M.A., The College of Staten Island)

Department of English
Moore High School
Staten Island, New York

Contents

Each section includes List of Characters, Summary, Analysis, Study Questions and Answers, and Suggested Essay Topics.

SECTION ONE

Introduction

The Life and Work of Joseph Conrad

In a part of Russia that once belonged to Poland, Joseph Conrad was born Josef Teodor Konrad Nalecz Korzeniowski on December 3, 1857 to his parents, Apollo and Evelina. Members of the landed gentry, his parents believed in liberating Poland, though from opposite extremes. Apollo Korzeniowski came from a family dedicated to the romantic idealism of their cause, eager to act, if necessary, to die for Poland. Though championing the same beliefs, Evelina Bobrowski's family advocated working quietly for their goal, and surviving as best they could under the dictates of the occupying power. Their concerns deeply influenced Conrad's upbringing.

Apollo devoted his life to literary interests and political involvement. He wrote plays and poems of little value, but adeptly translated Victor Hugo and Shakespeare into Polish. In 1862, Conrad's father started a literary journal, *Fortnightly Review*. Politically, Apollo's main concern centered around fortifying resistance against Russian oppression. He helped organize the National Central Committee. He joined a radical wing and was arrested before he took any action. Exiled to the Vologda region of northern Russia in 1862, Apollo longed to have his family accompany him.

Already physically fragile, Conrad's mother suffered under the harshness of exile. The strain of imprisonment hastened her death in 1865 at thirty-four, less than three years after their exile. Authorities allowed Apollo to move to southern Russia after his wife's death. Suffering from tuberculosis later in life, and not considered a threat anymore, Apollo returned home. He spent his last months in Cracow, where he died in 1869.

By the time Conrad was a teenager, he had suffered from his family's political involvement. At four, he saw his father arrested; at seven, he saw his mother die; and, at eleven, he saw his father die. He was left in the care of his uncle, Thaddeus Bobrowski. These traumatic experiences stayed with Conrad for his entire life. They fueled his wish to flee Poland. Consequently, they also instilled in him feelings of desertion, betrayal, and guilt for leaving his home-land. These themes were explored deeply in his work, *Lord Jim*.

From his parents' tribulations, Conrad concluded that no future lay in store for him in Poland. He needed to escape to fash-ion a life based on his inner promptings. His desire to see other countries led him to say as he looked at a map of Africa, "When I grow up I shall go there." That place was the Belgian Congo, which became the germ for *Heart of Darkness*.

By traveling, Conrad could secure economic independence, live out adventures, and escape political unrest. Since his uncle had connections in the shipping industry and French was his second language, the French merchant marine attracted him, even though he had never seen the sea. The excitement he had read about in the works of Victor Hugo and James Fenimore Cooper could now become part of his life. His Polish relatives viewed his choice of becoming a sailor as an insult to his cultural background.

Two months before his seventeenth birthday, in 1874, Conrad left for Marseilles and a sea career. The four years he spent on French ships gave him the richness of experience he longed for. He sailed to the West Indies, and Central and South America. On his second voyage, he met Spanish rebels and smuggled guns on their behalf. With his ship wrecked on the Spanish coast, Conrad escaped to France. He fictionalized these experiences in his novels *Nostromo* (1904) and *The Arrow of Gold* (1919).

At this time he met Dona Rita, a Spanish rebel. He supposedly fought a pistol duel with an American, Captain Blunt, over her. Both were wounded. Rita and Blunt disappeared by the time Thaddeus arrived. Conrad told his uncle he had lost money gambling and had tried to commit suicide, he said nothing about the duel. Here, his adventures in France ended.

After turning twenty, Conrad switched allegiances to Britain by becoming an English seaman. He did so for two reasons: he wanted to flee the obligation to the Russian military forces and he thought that if he learned English, he could be promoted sooner.

Modern British literature profited from Conrad's defection from the French seas. There is a good possibility he would not have undertaken his writing career in English if he had not joined the British navy. In 1886, the same year he was naturalized as a British citizen, Conrad passed his examinations for master mariner. By then it was clear his life had settled and he had made a wise choice.

Conrad served on British ships for nearly twelve years. As second mate, he sailed on a ship journeying between Singapore and Borneo. He sailed to the Orient on the *Palestine,* a ship that burned and sank off the coast of Java. He used this adventure in *Youth* (1902). In 1888, ten years after his switch from the French to British seas, he commanded his only ship, the *Otago.* His novella, *The Secret Sharer,* reflects this experience. His one interlude from the British service was when he piloted a river boat to the Belgian Congo, the basis for *Heart of Darkness.* This journey also affected his health, a consequence which may have influenced his switch from seaman to writer.

He began writing his first novel, *Almayer's Folly,* in 1889, though he did not in any way consider himself a writer. He eventually submitted the manuscript in 1894; it was accepted after Edward Garnett read it. Through Garnett's encouragement, Conrad began writing another novel. He still pursued a sea career, however, attempting to secure a command until 1898. For the next thirteen years, he wrote nearly one volume per year.

Married and with two sons, Conrad found it difficult to live off his literary earnings, even though he lived modestly in country homes. He received a Civil List pension from the British government.

After twenty years and sixteen volumes, Conrad finally achieved popular success with his novel *Chance* (1913). His limited audience grew to a wider acceptance.

During his literary career, Conrad met and made friends with Stephen Crane, H. G. Wells, Ford Madox Ford, and Henry James—influential writers of their time. Even with their friendships, he lived outside the mainstream of literary life. He was unaware of

Freud's work and other scientific advances. He knew nothing of James Joyce, Virginia Woolf, and D. H. Lawrence—writers with whom his work is often compared. Yet, his relative isolation did not prevent him from formulating his philosophy about art, fiction, and their relation to life. Many of the prefaces of his novels serve as his foundation for his artistic beliefs.

Often linked to Herman Melville and Jack London, other writers of adventure stories, Conrad infused his work with psychological and moral implications. His characters face deep problems, ones with difficult or no answers. Their response to these questions often determines the course of their lives. Symbol and myth fill his fiction, and much of his story lies beneath the surface narrative. The adventure is merely one level of the story, the more intriguing one is buried under the plot. Reading a work by Conrad requires patience, diligence, and concentration.

From his first book, he used "Joseph Conrad" as his writing name, his difficult given name had been misspelled too many times on official sailing papers. A master craftsman and stylist, Conrad labored at the writing process. No writing came easy to him. His major works include *Almayer's Folly* (1895), *The Nigger of the Narcissus* (1897), *Lord Jim* (1900), *Youth*—containing *Heart of Darkness* (1902), *Nostromo* (1904), *The Secret Agent* (1907), *The Secret Sharer* (1910), *Under Western Eyes* (1911), and *Victory* (1915).

Never a healthy man, Conrad suffered from indigestion, hypochondria, and melancholia. Conrad died at his desk in 1924, at the age of sixty-six. A man who did not speak English before he was twenty-two, and did not write English until he taught himself at thirty-two, Joseph Conrad fashioned his life at sea into his life in fiction. By transforming experience into art, he established his permanence as a twentieth-century British novelist.

Historical Background

Conrad based *Heart of Darkness* on his journey to the Belgian Congo in 1890. By checking his diaries at the time, we can trace his experience against his fictional portrayal. But this novella is more than an autobiographical account of his time spent there. It is a modern work that challenges the basic ethical question of good and evil in mankind, a topic explored by many authors. We need only think of the Adam and Eve myth, Milton's *Paradise Lost*, Dante's *Divine Comedy*, Golding's *Lord of the Flies,* and Burgess's *A Clockwork Orange* to name a few. Francis Ford Coppola based his film, *Apocalypse Now,* on this philosophical concept by updating Conrad's story to the Vietnam War and the Southeast Asian jungle of the 1960s.

Conrad also tackled the political environment of the Congo in *Heart of Darkness.* When King Leopold of Belgium founded the "International Association for the Suppression of Slavery and the Opening Up of Central Africa," he attempted to impose civilization and order. Greed, though, fostered widespread abuse. By the time Conrad visited the Congo, exploitation festered everywhere. Brutality and degradation reigned, not progress and enlightenment. The natives' sufferings and Kurtz's writings about them reflect the historical reality.

A number of factors influenced Conrad and other twentieth-century British writers. We have to first understand Victorian England and the reasons why the modern novelist rejected the values and beliefs of that time to mold a new society founded on different ideals.

Victorian England believed in materialism and progress. Their bourgeois (middle class) values served to stabilize all facets of society, so they believed. The writings of Jane Austen, Charles Dickens and George Eliot represented the standards of their time, with *Pride and Prejudice, Great Expectations,* and *Middlemarch* serving as landmarks in fiction at that time. Their novels usually followed the traditional three-volume format. They focussed on many details, often writing at length about seemingly insignificant details.

As the era closed, reaction against Victorian life, commercialism, and community spread. The artist stood, not as a member of society, but in isolation from it. Once embraced by authors, religious faith even declined.

With formal religion destroyed, writers needed to discover a new faith to follow—with art often filling the void. In his preface to *The Nigger of Narcissus*, Conrad wrote: "Art itself may be defined as a single-minded attempt to render the highest kind of justice to the visible universe, by bringing to light the truth, manifold and one, underlying its very aspect." For him, art was religion.

New techniques emerged for novelists to tell their stories. The stream of consciousness and internal monologue emphasized a shift in focus from the external world to the interior world. Dreams, thoughts, and explanations of a character's mental process replaced lengthy descriptions of external objects. Even though Conrad did not use these devices per se, he did focus on the internal world of his characters, and the reality of their dreams and thoughts. Marlow's story suggests a nightmarish journey into the unknown.

More than any other factor, the advent and progression of psychology shaped the new vision of man in the universe, as well as the artist's conception of him. Freud's ideas showed the different aspects of man's personality. With Freud's analysis, man is not easily understood unless we consider his multi-layered make-up. His terms "ego," "id," and "super-ego" reveal the depth of our conscious and subconscious mind. After Freud's work appeared, many works received a "psychological" interpretation. This added a depth of meaning to each work which had not existed before.

If we look at *Heart of Darkness* specifically and apply Freud's concept of the human psyche, we can analyze Marlow's journey not only as a literal one, but a psychological one. Marlow and Kurtz represent different aspects of man's personality. Marlow reflects the "ego" (man's more rational side), while Kurtz represents the "id" (man's primitive force within). This difference explains why Marlow recoils at Kurtz's barbaric behavior.

The recurring symbols in Conrad's work show Jung's influence. Many things represent not only their actual meaning, but a symbolic one, as well. The jungle, Marlow's journey, and even Kurtz himself suggest other ideas and meanings besides their literal ones. Since Conrad gives no clues, the reader must interpret each one.

Bergson's theories of time relate to Conrad's use of a non-chronological narration. He could have had Marlow tell his story without any alteration in time, by starting at the beginning and proceeding straight through until the end. Instead, Conrad lets Marlow jump ahead, then return at whim. This technique merges the past with the present, making the reading more challenging. It shuffles the pieces of a strict chronological plot. As with the symbols, the reader must order the time to organize the sequence of events.

In his preface to *The Nigger of the Narcissus*, Joseph Conrad wrote how an artist's (writer's) success allowed readers a "glimpse of truth for which you have forgotten to ask." He also said: "Art itself may be defined as a single-minded attempt to render the highest kind of justice to the visible universe, by bringing to light the truth, manifold and one, underlying its every aspect." In each case, notice his reference to the "truth." Here, Conrad proclaimed what his contemporaries felt. Only the artist could lead society to the truth. Only the work itself could enable society to understand the truth. The modern artists stood before their audience like prophets addressing the multitudes. The twentieth-century novelists' work represented a way for the reader to see the new reality.

Master List of Characters

"I"—*An unnamed "I" narrator.*

The Director of Companies—*Captain and owner of the boat.*

The Lawyer and The Accountant—*People on the boat in the Thames.*

Charlie Marlow—*Also on the boat. Tells the story of his journey to see Kurtz deep in the jungle.*

Kurtz—*The manager of an ivory station who has rejected conventional societal beliefs.*

Two Knitting Women—*They sit outside the outer office.*

The Doctor—*He examines Marlow before his journey.*

The Aunt—*Related to Marlow, she helps him get the appointment to the ship.*

The Swedish Captain—*The man in charge of a little sea-going steamer.*

The Accountant—*The bookkeeper who draws attention because of his neat appearance.*

The Dying Agent—*The man tormented by flies at the station.*

The Manager—*Leader of the station who survives because of his excellent health.*

The Pilgrims—*Workers who carry long staves. They want any chance to obtain ivory.*

The Brickmaker—*He does secretarial work for the Manager, but doesn't seem to make bricks.*

The Boilermaker—*A good worker who talks to Marlow about the rivets they need.*

The Manager's Uncle—*The leader of the Eldorado Exploring Expedition. He only talks to his nephew.*

The Helmsman—*A black man killed by arrows shot by the natives.*

The Russian—*Wearing bright colored clothes, he greets Marlow at Kurtz's station.*

Kurtz's Black Mistress—*The woman in the jungle. She wears many bracelets, charms, and beads.*

A Clean-Shaved Man, Kurtz's "Cousin," a Journalist—*Three men who visit Marlow after Kurtz's death. They want Kurtz's papers.*

Kurtz's Intended—*The woman in Europe who Marlow visits a year after Kurtz's death.*

Summary of the Novel

Five men sit on board the *Nellie*, a boat docked in the Thames. An unnamed narrator introduces them to the reader: the owner of the boat, a lawyer, an accountant, and Charlie Marlow, who tells the story of his journey to the African jungle.

He introduces his tale by referring to ancient times in Britain, some nineteen hundred years ago. After help from an aunt, Marlow gets a job commanding a ship for an ivory trading company. Before he leaves, he meets two knitting women and a doctor from the company who make him feel uneasy.

He sails from Europe on a French steamer. The endless coastline and the appearance of sweating and shouting black men fascinate him. After more than thirty days, he leaves the French steamer for a boat captained by a Swede. He makes it to the company's Outer

Station. Rotting equipment and black slaves chained by the neck appall him. Even when he runs from the sight of them, he sees black workers starving and dying slowly. He meets the company's chief accountant, a man whose neat appearance stands out from the company's chaos. He waits ten days here. The hot weather and many flies irritate Marlow. During this time, though, the accountant mentions Mr. Kurtz, a remarkable man, a first-class ivory agent, a favorite of the Administration.

Marlow leaves the Outer Station with a white companion and a caravan of sixty blacks. Through thickets, ravines, and paths they travel two-hundred miles in fifteen days to the Central Station. Marlow finds his steamboat sunk at the bottom of the river. It will take months to repair. He meets the manager, a man Marlow dislikes because he talks without thinking. He speaks of Kurtz, saying he is ill, perhaps dead. Like the accountant, the manager praises Kurtz and reiterates his importance to the company. Marlow turns his back on the manager and concentrates on repairing his steamboat. Everywhere he looks, he notices "pilgrims," white men who carry staves and speak of nothing but ivory. A shed full of goods burns one night. While going to see it, Marlow overhears the manager speaking with another agent about Kurtz.

Marlow meets a brickmaker. He invites Marlow to his room, where he asks him many questions about Europe. As he leaves the room, Marlow sees a sketch in oils of a blindfolded woman carrying a torch. Kurtz had painted it, he says, more than a year ago.

They talk about Kurtz, the agent saying he expects him to be promoted soon. He says Kurtz and Marlow belong to the same "gang" because the same people had recommended both of them. Marlow realizes this man resents Kurtz's success.

Marlow tells the agent he needs rivets to fix the boat. When Marlow finally demands the rivets, the agent abruptly changes the subject. They do not arrive for many weeks. Marlow boards his steamer after the agent leaves. He meets a boilermaker, a good worker with a long beard. They dance on deck after Marlow tells him the rivets will come soon. Led by the manager's uncle, the Eldorado Exploring Expedition appears. Marlow overhears them speak about Kurtz. He had come downriver a few months ago with ivory, but turned back. He had left a clerk to deliver the shipment, instead. He had spoken of Kurtz's illness then, with no further word coming in the last nine months.

The rivets arrive, Marlow repairs the boat, and they resume the journey. The manager, a few pilgrims, and twenty natives accompany Marlow on the steamer. It takes two months to get close to Kurtz's station. During that time, drums roll, people howl and clap, and the jungle becomes thick and dark.

They find an abandoned hut fifty-miles below Kurtz's station. Marlow discovers a faded note, a coverless book, and a stack of firewood. Eight miles from Kurtz's station, Marlow and the manager argue over their navigation. Marlow wants to push on, but the manager urges caution. A mile and a half from their destination, the natives attack the boat. A spear kills the helmsman, who falls at Marlow's feet. They throw his body into the river, a simple funeral. They come upon a man on shore. A Russian, this "harlequin" speaks admiringly of Kurtz. He tells them of Kurtz's serious illness.

While the manager and the pilgrims go to Kurtz's house, Marlow finds out many things from the Russian about Kurtz. Kurtz had ordered the attack on the steamer, he had discovered villages, and had even tried to kill the Russian over some ivory. Most importantly, the natives worshipped Kurtz, and offered sacrifices in his name.

They bring Kurtz to the steamer on an improvised stretcher. Physically weak, Kurtz still speaks with power. The natives line the shore to watch their god leave. A black woman, Kurtz's mistress, joins them. Kurtz escapes from the steamer that evening. Marlow follows him, finally returning Kurtz to the boat. Kurtz gives Marlow a packet of papers. He dies a few days later. His last words—"The horror! The horror!"—haunt Marlow. They bury him in a muddy hole the next day.

Marlow returns to Europe. He becomes sick, running a fever. Three people call on him to retrieve Kurtz's writings. A company officer, a musician claiming to be Kurtz's cousin, and a journalist want his papers for their use. Marlow gives them unimportant documents, saving the personal ones for Kurtz's Intended.

More than a year after Kurtz's death, Marlow visits this woman. At her door, he hears Kurtz's last words ring. In a drawing room,

Marlow meets her, a beautiful lady suffering over Kurtz's death. Marlow never answers her questions directly. He lies to her, saying Kurtz's last words were her name. She cries to release herself from the agony of loss. Marlow feels bad for betraying Kurtz's memory, but glad for saving the woman from the truth.

With Marlow's story ended, we return to the *Nellie*. The narrator describes Marlow sitting in the pose of a Buddha, then raises his head to the "heart of the immense darkness" in the distance.

Estimated Reading Time

Due to Conrad's complex language, the long paragraphs, and the chronological shifts in narration, *Heart of Darkness* will probably take longer to cover than another work of equal length, with an actual reading time of six to seven hours.

SECTION TWO

Heart of Darkness

Section I (pages 1-27)

New Characters:

The Director of Companies: *captain and owner of the boat*

"I": *unnamed narrator on the boat*

The Lawyer, The Accountant: *people on the boat in the Thames*

Charlie Marlow: *also on the boat; tells the story of his journey to see Kurtz deep in the jungle*

Two Knitting Women: *they sit outside the outer office*

The Doctor: *he examines Marlow before his journey*

The Aunt: *related to Marlow, she helps him get his appointment to the ship*

The Swedish Captain: *the man in charge of a little sea-going steamer*

The Company's Chief Accountant: *his neat appearance contrasts with the chaos of the station*

The Dying Agent: *the man tormented by flies at the station*

The Manager: *leader of the station who survives because of his excellent health*

The Pilgrims: *workers who carry long staves; they want any chance to obtain ivory*

The Brickmaker: *does secretarial work for the manager, but does not seem to make bricks*

The Boilermaker: *a good worker who talks to Marlow about the rivets they need*

The Manager's Uncle: *leader of the Eldorado Exploring Expedition; he speaks only to his nephew*

Summary

A boat, the *Nellie*, is docked in the Thames. Its sails are still, and the water and sea calm. An unnamed narrator, who refers to himself only as "I," introduces the people on board. Four people sit on deck besides himself: the Director of Companies, the Lawyer, the Accountant, and Marlow. The Director of Companies is their captain and host. An elderly man, the Lawyer, sits on the rug for comfort, while the Accountant plays with a box of dominoes. Finally, Marlow sits cross-legged, his arms dropped, his palms facing outward. The narrator says they "exchanged a few words lazily."

The unnamed narrator thinks of the great history of the sea, its people, and ships. He mentions Sir Francis Drake and Sir John Franklin. He recalls the *Golden Hind*, the *Erebus*, and the *Terror*—ships from the past. He mentions all the greatness, dreams, and empires of history.

The sun sets. In the distance, the lights from the Chapman lighthouse, ships, and London shine at night. Still, a lurid glare glows between London and the sky.

Marlow speaks about London, saying how it's been "one of the dark places of the earth." No one responds. The narrator tells us that Marlow is the only one who still follows the sea. He considers him to be a wanderer. Their home is the ship, their country is the sea. He says Marlow is not typical. For Marlow, when he tells a tale, its meaning is not inside like a kernel, but outside.

Suddenly, Marlow begins talking about the Romans and ancient times. He pictures the cold, fog, disease, and battles with the savage natives they had to endure. He admires their courage to face the darkness. In the posture of a Buddha, he speaks about how they used only force and violence to get what they wanted. Conquests back then, he says, meant stealing from people who were different from you. He believes there is more needed to redeem mankind, something to "bow down before, and offer a sacrifice to…."

Marlow stops speaking. There is a long silence and no one speaks. When he starts talking again, he begins to tell a story of one of his journeys. He says it reveals something about himself.

Marlow tells of how he'd spent six years traveling on the Indian Ocean, Pacific, and China Seas before taking the journey he's talking about. When he was young, he used to point to blank spaces on maps and say, "When I grow up I will go there." He's visited most of them, except one. He calls Africa a "place of darkness." He compares the Congo river on the map to a snake: its head in the sea, its body curving over a country, and its tail in the deep of the land. As he had looked at a map in a shop window, he says he was as fascinated by this place as a bird is when it looks at a snake.

He cannot secure this job until his aunt helps him. She knows the wife of a person in the Administration. Marlow cannot believe he needs help from a woman.

Marlow tells how the company had recently discovered the death of one of their captains by a native. His name was Fresleven and his murder stemmed from an argument over some black hens. Months later, when Marlow arrives, he uncovers Fresleven's body, the grass growing over his remains.

In forty-eight hours Marlow crosses the Channel and presents himself to his employer. Knitting black wool, two women—one fat, the other thin—sit outside the office. A map on a wall pictures the world in many colors. Marlow mentions the yellow patch at dead center, his destination.

Marlow meets the secretary, signs his contract, and is told he must have a medical exam. The women continue knitting as he passes through the outer office. They watch him strangely. A young clerk shows Marlow out of the office. It is early for his exam, so Marlow and the clerk have a drink. Speaking admiringly of Africa, the clerk surprises Marlow by not going there himself. "I am not such a fool as I look," he says. At his exam, the doctor measures Marlow's head with calipers. He asks if there was any madness in Marlow's family. He also adds, "…the changes take place inside, you know."

Marlow visits his aunt to thank her and say good-bye. He finds that his aunt had recommended him as "an emissary of light, something like a lower apostle." All woman are out of touch with the truth, he says. He feels hesitant about leaving Brussels for Africa, the "center of the earth." He leaves on a slow French steamer. It stops at many ports to unload soldiers and officers. The monotonous journey lulls Marlow into a depression. Occasionally, a boat from shore paddled by blacks interrupts the boredom. The steamer passes a French man-of-war ship shelling the coastline. They deliver mail to this ship. They also learn that the sailors aboard her were dying of fever at three a day. The steamer moves on, never stopping for Marlow to get a clear impression, except for "hints of nightmares." They reach the mouth of the river in thirty days. Marlow switches to a small sea-going steamer captained by a Swede to take him farther upstream. The captain tells him he had taken a fellow Swede recently up the river. The man had hanged himself. The captain cannot answer Marlow directly when he asks why. When they reach the Outer Station, Marlow gets his first glimpse of Africa, the ivory trade, and the general waste. Broken machinery and loose rails litter the ground. Commanded by an arrogant guard, a six-man chain gang walks by with the "deathlike indifference of unhappy savages."

Shocked, Marlow turns away from them and heads for the trees. Marlow avoids an artificial hole and nearly falls into a narrow ravine before reaching the shade. Black shapes occupy the area. These diseased, starving men lean against trees. Marlow gives one young man a biscuit he had gotten from the Swede's ship. He takes it, but does not eat it. Another man crawls to the river to drink.

Marlow walks away from the station. He meets a white man whose fanciful appearance contrasts with the surrounding darkness. He is the Company's chief accountant. Everything about him is orderly, unlike the "muddle" around him.

Marlow spends ten days at the Outer Station. Flies buzz. A deathly sick agent is brought in. He groans continuously. A caravan also arrives. The ensuing uproar causes the accountant to say he hates the savages "to the death." With sixty men, Marlow leaves the next day for the Central Station. He has a white companion, a man who faints and catches fever. Marlow meets a white man in an unbuttoned uniform. He says he repairs roads, but Marlow sees no roads or upkeep.

After fifteen days, Marlow reaches the Central Station. He finds that the boat he was to command was wrecked at the bottom of the river. The repair job, he knows, will take months. Marlow meets the manager in a curious interview. This man has attained his position because of his good health, not his ability and performance. The manager tells Marlow he had wanted to wait for him two days before, but he couldn't because Kurtz, the Inner Station's manager, was ill. He had visited him, and the skipper of Marlow's boat tore the bottom out. Marlow says he has heard of Kurtz. The manager assures Marlow of Kurtz's value. He also adds that it will take three months to repair the boat. Disgusted, Marlow leaves angered with the manager. He sees "pilgrims," white men carrying staves. A bit later, a shed full of prints, beads, and other goods catches fire. Marlow investigates the scene. He hears two men talking. One mentions Kurtz. The other is the manager. A black man accused of starting the fire is beaten. The "brickmaker" invites Marlow to his room for a drink. Marlow does not see a "fragment of a brick anywhere." He asks Marlow about Europe and his connections there. Marlow realizes the man intends to get information. Marlow notices a sketch in oils on the wall. It is of a "woman, draped and blindfolded, carrying a lighted torch." The manager says Kurtz had painted it a year before at the Central Station.

Marlow asks about Kurtz. The manager calls Kurtz a "prodigy," and an "emissary of pity and science and progress…." He says the same people who had sent Kurtz also had recommended Marlow. They go outside. A man with a black mustache approves of beating the black native blamed for the fire. The agent follows Marlow. He doesn't want Marlow to speak badly of him to Kurtz. Marlow detests this man who, he thinks, has "nothing inside but a little loose dirt, maybe." Marlow adds how he hates a lie because it appalls him. He also says it is hard for one person to explain himself to another because, "We live, as we dream—alone."

Momentarily, the story returns to the *Nellie*. The narrator listens intently, though the others may have been sleeping. It is dark. Marlow is more voice than person.

Marlow resumes his story. The brickmaker continues speaking of Kurtz, calling him a "universal genius." Marlow demands rivets to repair the boat. Every week, a caravan arrives with trade goods, but never any rivets. The man says Kurtz, too, needs rivets. Marlow suggests that, as secretary to the manager, he should find a way to obtain them. The man mentions a hippopotamus, then leaves.

Marlow needs rivets to continue. He says he does not like to work, but enjoys finding himself, his "own reality," while working. He returns to the boat. He speaks with the foreman, a man Marlow admires because of his dedication to work. A widower with six young children, this man raves about pigeons. He tells the man that rivets will arrive in a few weeks. They dance with joy on the deck.

The rivets do not come for awhile. An exploring party, the Eldorado Exploring Expedition, arrives. For the next six weeks, they appear in sections. A white man on a donkey leads each group, followed by a band of blacks. They are reckless, greedy, and cruel. They will "tear treasure out of the bowels of the land."

The manager's uncle leads them. Fat, with short legs, he resembles a butcher. He speaks only to his nephew. They stay together all day with their heads close to one another.

Analysis

Conrad uses a "framed" narrative technique. One narrator, in this case "I," sets up another narrator, Marlow, who will continue the story. At first, readers may suspect that "I" will narrate the story. He doesn't. After introducing the passengers to us, Marlow talks. His story becomes *Heart of Darkness*. Conrad reveals some of "I's" thoughts to us, then Marlow's story takes over.

The reader should remember that Marlow's journey has already happened. He is not actually experiencing the events as he speaks of them. Marlow also abandons chronological sequence. Sometimes he jumps ahead in his story, then retraces his narration.

Conrad establishes a calm gloominess at the beginning. The *Nellie* is "without a flutter of sails," "the wind was nearly calm," and the air "seemed condensed into a mournful gloom." Later, when the sun sets, there is still a "brooding gloom in the sunshine." These descriptions suggest an eerie setting, as if something evil is about to occur. The narrator says the passengers feel "the bond of the sea" between them. We see this shared feeling when the narrator thinks of the sea's history on the Thames, and Marlow speaks of the Romans nineteen hundred years ago. The past interests them. Marlow's idea of history, though, includes the savages in Ancient Rome and "aggravated murder on a great scale." The dark side intrigues him. His first sentence contains the words "dark places." Even the river on a map resembles a snake, a sinister reptile.

Conrad deepens Marlow's uniqueness with his physical posture. He sits cross-legged in "the pose of a Buddha preaching in European clothes." Very simply, Buddhist philosophy establishes suffering as inseparable from existence. It also contains "nirvana," a state of illumination. If he imitates a Buddha, how has Marlow suffered and what does he know?

He refers to the company he will join when he calls them "conquerors," people who "grabbed what they could get for the sake of what was to be got." He disapproves of them. Since they did not have "belief in the idea," Marlow rejects their ambitions as a mere materialistic hunt.

As the traffic in London continues, the narrator mentions the green, red, and white flames gliding in the river during the "deepening night." Again, images of light and dark play against each other.

In order for Marlow to convey meaning in his tale, he says he must tell us how he got there, what he saw, and how he went up the river to meet the "poor chap," Kurtz. The journey was not "very clear," but it seemed to "throw a kind of light." In a symbolic way now, dark and light mix. Marlow relates his feelings as a child, when he used to stare at maps and dream of explorations. Since then, many of those places had been visited, named, and inhabited. One place remains, though—the river "resembling an immense snake uncoiled." Traditionally, snakes symbolize evil. Marlow speaks of it with this meaning, saying the place "had become a place of darkness." This refers to the Belgian Congo.

Marlow tells how he needed help from his aunt to secure his appointment. He says, "Then would you believe it?—I tried the women. I, Charlie Marlow, set the women to work—to get a job.

Heavens!" This information seems insignificant. It isn't. Conrad foreshadows Marlow's lie to Kurtz's Intended at the end of the novel. He will sacrifice the truth for a woman.

Our first indication of wasteful suffering during Marlow's journey comes when he mentions Fresleven's death. Killed in a fight over two black hens, the captain's murder suggests an abandonment of rational behavior. Since Marlow has been to the jungle, he says it "didn't surprise me in the least to hear this." No respect is even shown to Fresleven's corpse, because Marlow discovers his body with grass growing over it.

The two knitting women present another sign of the macabre. Marlow thinks of them "guarding the door of Darkness, knitting black wool as for a warm pall…" Everything about them gives him an "eerie feeling."

Marlow's visit to the doctor adds to the idea on the unknown. The doctor measures his head, then asks if there was any sign of madness in Marlow's family. He also says the changes take place "inside." These clues lead us to believe that Marlow's journey is more than a physical one, it is a mental and psychological one.

Marlow knows what happens, but he has not told us yet. Conrad withholds information to create suspense. Though short, Marlow's visit to his aunt contains an important passage. She had recommended him, Marlow believes, using the words "emissary of light." This connects to a scene later in Section I, when the manager refers to Kurtz as an "emissary." They share the description of being a messenger or agent. We cannot know their message, though, until Marlow concludes his story.

The beginning of Marlow's journey on the French steamer initiates his descent into "darkness." They travel on the "edge of a colossal jungle, so dark as to be almost black…." At this point, light still shows. The sun is "fierce," the land "seemed to glisten," and "grayish-whitish specks showed up clustered inside the white surf." Conrad alternates images of light and darkness not only to convey mood, but to allude to ethical questions of good and bad, and right and wrong. As Marlow's journey progresses though, light fades and darkness dominates.

The Swede's story of a fellow Swede's suicide advances the idea of irrational acts. Marlow is not told the reason why he had hanged himself. We can sense the feeling of chaos Marlow will find in Africa. Why is there killing and madness? Notice how Conrad hints at these strange events without actually revealing too much about them.

Marlow notices more decay. He sees an "undersized railway truck lying on its back," the "carcass of some animal," and "a stack of rusty nails." These images define a general sense of squalor, a sign of neglect and waste. As Marlow tells of his travels, he never fails to include these descriptions. He has seen a world few of us have.

The next scene, when Marlow sees the black slaves chained together, shows us his disgust of man's treatment toward his fellow man. Here, Conrad attacks imperialism—the use by one group or nation over another for their own gain. The whites in the jungle use the blacks, reducing them to machines. Marlow feels guilty of this attitude, saying he is "a part of the great cause of these high and just proceedings." He flees from them to disassociate himself from the treatment of the blacks. But Marlow cannot run away. Everywhere, starving and dying blacks lean for rest, crawl for water, and crouch for shade. Marlow is "horrorstruck." The savage cruelty reflects the depravity in the jungle. And, he has only begun his journey.

The appearance of the Company's chief accountant represents a sharp contrast. His "brushed hair," "starched collars," and "got-up shirt-fronts" show a sense of order amidst all disorder. Marlow acknowledges him. While all around the manager falls to waste and rots, he keeps himself and his books in "apple-pie order." He cannot tolerate the groans of a dying agent in his office because it makes it "difficult to guard against clerical errors."

Marlow hears of Kurtz for the first time. The manager praises him. Marlow knows nothing of him at this time. Remember, in reality, Marlow knows everything about Kurtz because he is recounting the events, not experiencing them now.

The next part of Marlow's journey, with a caravan of sixty men, leads him through "networks of paths." No people are around, "nobody, not a hut." He sees "abandoned villages" and "ruins of grass walls." The jungle gets darker, the isolation more pronounced. The "white men with long staves" in their hands who appear momentarily represent the "pilgrims," the ivory hunters. They seek money and profit. They ignore the degradation. Marlow's meeting with the manager here serves three purposes: he finds out that the steamer he is to command is stuck, he hears more about Kurtz, and he comes to dislike this man because he is a "chattering idiot." The manager's superior health contrasts with the information about Kurtz's illness. We should observe how Conrad's conception of health includes the physical and mental. The jungle, its weather, and isolation affect everyone in many ways. The accountant and this manager seem to have survived the conditions. Others succumb. Which group will Marlow and Kurtz belong to? The manager is an interesting character. He seems to hate Kurtz. If Marlow and Kurtz are linked together, then he must hate Marlow. This explains why Marlow is uneasy around him.

Marlow feels that the manager can only "keep the routine going—that's all." The manager never offers food or rest to Marlow. "Being hungry," he says, "and kept on my feet too, I was getting savage." The key word is, of course, "savage." Are the surroundings influencing Marlow? And if the manager praises Kurtz, but Marlow dislikes the manager, can he accept his assessment of Kurtz?

Marlow sees more "pilgrims," who speak of ivory. The word "rang in the air, was whispered, was sighed." He detests this greed for wealth. He considers it to be "philanthropic pretense." Unconcerned with money, Marlow is the outsider, the intruder.

The brickmaker's appearance poses an intriguing question. How can he be a brickmaker if there are no bricks around? He fits the man who repairs roads earlier in the section, when Marlow said he did not see roads or upkeep. A mysterious element surrounds many characters. It is difficult to get a sense of them. Conrad leaves us questioning both who these people are, and Marlow's description of them. Are they the way Marlow describes them, or is he purposely omitting important information about them? If he is, then why? Conrad raises these questions through the use of the first-person flashback narrative.

Marlow's description of Kurtz's oil painting gives us the first solid detail about him. The picture of a woman draped and blindfolded carrying a lighted torch against a black background suggests a few ideas. First, we see the combination of light and dark again. The blindfold refers to the actual darkness, as well as a spiritual and philosophical one, since the person cannot "see." The woman anticipates Kurtz's mistress and Intended, two women who will appear later.

In the next sequence, Marlow reveals much about his philosophy. He says he hates and detests a lie. Again, Conrad foreshadows the ending, when Marlow lies to Kurtz's Intended. Later, we have to compare that moment with this statement. Marlow then says it is difficult for him to convey Kurtz to his listeners, the people on the boat. This implies us, the reader, also. "Do you see him? Do you see the story? Do you see anything? It seems to me I am trying to tell you a dream." he says. This points to Marlow's problem. He is trying to tell the untellable, explain the unexplainable. Marlow's words reflect Conrad's function as a writer—to make the reader understand the story. "We live, as we dream—alone." Marlow adds. This statement comes close to illuminating Marlow's tale. It is extremely difficult, if not impossible, for one person to understand another.

If this is true, then Marlow cannot understand Kurtz, Kurtz cannot understand Marlow, and we cannot understand either of them. We can try to make sense, nothing more. As Marlow's tale becomes philosophical, Conrad takes us back to the *Nellie* and the "I" narrator. This breaks the dream-like trance of the story. We come back to reality, if only for a moment. Everyone but the narrator is asleep. If we are like him, then we are "on watch for the sentence, for the word, that would give…the clue" to this story. Together, we try to catch Marlow's meaning.

Conrad returns to Marlow's story and a most practical matter: the need for rivets. Without them, his journey ends. This leads to a humorous scene when Marlow meets the Boilermaker, one of the few men he admires in the jungle. They reassure themselves that the rivets will arrive in three weeks, then danced "like lunatics."

The Eldorado Exploring Expedition arrives. Marlow abhors them. They want to "tear treasure out of the bowels of the land." They represent the greedy white men, whose sole purpose revolves around destroying the land to obtain money and wealth. Since the manager's uncle leads them, they further the idea of the pilgrims' infiltration. They lack "moral purpose," something Marlow appreciates.

Instead, Marlow thinks of Kurtz, a man "who had come out equipped with moral ideas of some sort." His interest stimulated, Marlow begins the next step on his quest to the mysterious ivory agent and the heart of darkness, a mythical place of hell.

Study Questions

1. Identify the people on the *Nellie*.

2. Why is it ironic that Marlow needs his aunt's help to secure his appointment?

3. What happened to Fresleven, one of the Company's captains?

4. How are the two women outside the secretary's office symbolic?

5. Name two unusual procedures at Marlow's physical exam.

6. How did the Swede die?

7. What is unique about the chief accountant's appearance?

8. Why was the manager successful at his job?

9. Why does Marlow call some people on the boat "pilgrims"?

10. Why does Marlow need the brickmaker's help?

Answers

1. A narrator, a company director, a lawyer, an accountant, and Marlow are aboard the *Nellie*.

2. It is ironic that Marlow needs his aunt's help because she is a woman in a male-dominated world, the sea.

3. Fresleven was murdered by a native in a quarrel over black hens.

4. The women outside the secretary's office knit black wool, the symbol of death.

5. The doctor measures Marlow's head with calipers, and asks if there has been madness in his family.

6. The Swede hanged himself.

7. The chief accountant is neat and orderly.

8. The manager was successful because he was always healthy.

9. Marlow calls them "pilgrims" because they carry staves and their "pilgrimage" is to obtain ivory.

10. Marlow need rivets from the brickmaker to repair the boat.

Suggested Essay Topics

1. From the very opening on the Thames in *Heart of Darkness*, when day mixes with night, Conrad uses images of light and dark. Traditionally, light represents "good" and dark represents "bad." Does Conrad use these interpretations in the same way? What do his constant references to light and dark suggest about Marlow's story? Remember, Africa is the "dark continent," where the black natives live.

2. Conrad alters his narration by making Marlow jump back and forth in time. Marlow mentions people and events we won't know about until later. Cite examples when he does this, and explain how it affects the story. What advantages are there in breaking the sequence of events? Why does he tell us some things, while withholding others?

3. In a sense, two narrators speak—a nameless "I" and Charlie Marlow. The narrator introduces Marlow, then tells us some of his ideas. When Marlow speaks, we see everything from his perspective. Suppose someone else told Marlow's story? Say, perhaps, the narrator or, possibly, one of the people Marlow meets along his journey. How would the story change? Would the information and details be different?

4. After taking the steamer captained by the Swede, Marlow sees the blacks for the first time. Why does the sight of them appall him? Why is he bothered by the way they are treated? No one else seems to be disturbed by their condition, so why is Marlow?

5. Section I contains a number of shorter episodes, as Marlow switches steamers and heads deeper into the jungle. What does he see and experience at each temporary stop over? Is there a progression as he moves from one boat to another? Does each stop affect Marlow's attitude and opinion toward what he sees?

SECTION THREE

Heart of Darkness

Section II (pages 27–50)

New Characters:

The Helmsman: *a black man killed by arrows shot by natives*

The Russian: *man who greets Marlow at Kurtz's station*

Summary

While on his boat, Marlow hears the manager and his uncle talk about Kurtz. They stand on the shore alongside the steamboat. Without moving, he listens. The manager fears Kurtz's influence. Threatened by Kurtz's influence and success, the manager says, "Am I the manager—or am I not?" The uncle hopes the climate will eventually ruin Kurtz.

From the "absurd sentences," Marlow hears how Kurtz had traveled three hundred miles with a shipment of ivory nine months ago. Kurtz had then returned upriver in a canoe with four native paddlers, a "half-caste" left in charge of delivering the load of ivory. Kurtz's station has been without goods and stores since then. Kurtz's motives escape the manager and his uncle. Marlow says he sees Kurtz in his mind for the first time, how he faces the wilderness and desolation. The half-caste, a "scoundrel" to the manager and his uncle, had told of Kurtz's illness and how he had "recovered imperfectly." They walk away from Marlow, then return close to the boat again. When they speak this time, Marlow is not sure if they are talking about Kurtz, or about someone else in Kurtz's district of whom the manager disapproves. The manager says neither of them will be free until "one of these fellows is hanged." They agree that the real danger begins in Europe, where the orders come from. The manager quotes something Kurtz had said: "Each station should be like a beacon on the road towards better things, a center for trade of course, but also for humanizing, improving, instructing." He calls Kurtz an "ass" for his ideas and his desire to be a manager one day. The uncle reassures his nephew when he says, "…I say, trust to this." He points to the jungle around him while he speaks, as if to say all these things will help you destroy Kurtz. Marlow jumps up to look at the forest, half expecting to receive an answer from the darkness. They knew he had been listening, he says, because they went back to the station "pretending not to know anything of my existence." Side by side, they walk away, their unequal shadows trailing behind them. The Eldorado Expedition leaves for the wilderness a few days later. In the future, Marlow finds out all the donkeys died, as well as the blacks, "the less valuable animals."

Marlow is excited about meeting Kurtz soon. It will not happen for two more months, though. They encounter warm air, empty streams, and the deep forest as they travel upriver. Marlow compares it to going back to the beginning of the world. Hippos and alligators line the sand-banks. Stillness and silence brood over everything. He has to watch for hidden banks to avoid damaging the boat. He looks for wood to burn for the next day's steaming. He refers to the details of his job as "monkey tricks," as the mysterious Truth watches him. He says when you attend to things on the surface, reality fades. The inner truth, he adds, is "hidden—luckily."

For a moment, we return to the men aboard the *Nellie*. One man says, "Try to be civil, Marlow." The narrator knows one person besides himself is listening. Driving the boat, Marlow says, resuming his story, was like a "blindfolded man set to drive a van over a bad road." He sweats and shivers over worrying about the boat. Once, he needs twenty cannibals to help push the boat. With sarcasm and humor, he says they at least did not "eat each other before my face." He recalls the smell of rotten hippo-meat the cannibals had brought with them. With the manager and three or four pilgrims holding their staves aboard, they pass white men greeting them with joy about ivory, the word itself ringing in the air. Massive trees fill the immense landscape. Marlow's journey is now headed "towards Kurtz—exclusively." He is not sure who it crawls to for the pilgrims. He hears the roll of drums, but does not understand if they signify war, peace, or prayer. The snapping of a twig can shatter the stillness of dawn. He again compares his journey to prehistoric times. Ancient man curses, prays, and welcomes them. Like phantoms, they glide past their surroundings. When natives howl and leap, Marlow thinks not how different they are from him, but their "remote kinship" to him. He says it is "ugly," if you are at least willing to admit it. He philosophizes about man's mind, and how it encompasses all periods of time and knowledge. Man must meet the truth with his own strength, not an external force.

Someone on the *Nellie* grunts a question. Marlow answers by saying he did not go ashore because he had to worry about the steampipes and the boat. Marlow mentions the fireman, a black man who keeps fire in the boiler. He could have been on shore with the natives, but instead helps Marlow because he has been trained for a profession. His filed teeth, strange patterns shaved on his head, and three scars on each of his cheeks fit well with his belief that an evil spirit lived inside the boiler. Both Marlow and the fireman are too busy with their jobs to think about their "creepy thoughts."

Marlow reaches a reed hut fifty miles below the Inner Station, Kurtz's domain. He finds a stack of firewood and a note: "Wood for you. Hurry up. Approach cautiously." Marlow knows something is wrong, but is not sure what. They look into the jungle, but find no clues. In the hut, with a plank on two posts serving as a table and rubbish in a dark corner, he finds a coverless book, *An Inquiry into some Points of Seamanship* . He handles it with care, even though it is not an "enthralling book." Marlow appreciates the work and concern required to write it. Finding the book and looking at the notes in cipher along the margin equal an "extravagant mystery" for Marlow.

While absorbed with the book, Marlow forgets the forest, the manager, and woodpile. When he looks up, everything has gone. The pilgrims shout at him, as he puts the book in his pocket. The boat is loaded and ready to go. The manager calls the white man who had lived in the hut an "intruder." He assumes he is English, but this will not protect him from trouble unless he is careful. No one in the world is safe from trouble, Marlow observes with "assumed innocence."

Convinced the more rapid current will overpower the steamer, Marlow expects the boat to give "her last gasp." Somehow, though, it moves on. Marlow thinks of what he will say to Kurtz when he meets him. Then he experiences a "flash of insight," and realizes the importance of this affair is under the surface, beyond his understanding.

In two days they are eight miles from Kurtz's station. The manager suggests they wait until morning for safety. Annoyed, Marlow reasons that one more night means little after so many months. The unnatural silence makes him believe he is deaf. At three in the morning, fish leap, their splash reminding Marlow of gun fire. Fog accompanies the rising sun. It lifts by eight or nine in the morning. He orders the anchor, which they were taking in, to be paid out again. A clamor "modulated in savage discords" through the air. It ends in a shriek, then stops, leaving silence. Frightened, the pilgrims rush for their guns—Winchesters. They anticipate an attack.

Marlow notices the different expressions on the whites and blacks aboard the ship. The whites look discomposed, shocked at the frightful noise. Though interested, the blacks remain calm. They grunt to each other. One black man says they should catch the people hiding in the jungle. When Marlow asks why, he says, "Eat 'im!" Bothered at first by this idea, Marlow figures they are hungry. Besides some rations they had brought aboard, they had taken only rotten hippo-meat, which the pilgrims had thrown overboard. In theory, Marlow says, they were to use their payment—three nine-inch pieces of brass—to purchase food at the villages. They could not, though, because there were no villages, the people were hostile, or the manager did not want to stop. Sarcastically, Marlow says they could have eaten the wire itself for food. Marlow wonders why the cannibals do not eat the five white men. They could have easily overpowered them. Something had restrained them, but Marlow is not sure what. He and the others look "unwholesome" and "unappetizing," he concludes. He also believes starvation is easier to fight than "bereavement, dishonor, and perdition of one's soul…." Fighting hunger requires all of a man's strength.

The manager wants to push on. Marlow knows they cannot steer properly. The manager authorizes him to "take all the risks." Marlow refuses. The manager defers to his judgment. Marlow turns away from the manager to look into the fog. He compares the adventures in approaching Kurtz to an "enchanted princess sleeping in a fabulous castle." The manager fears an attack. Marlow believes the thick fog will prevent it. He associates "sorrow" with the natives, not violence. Marlow feels the pilgrims stare at him as if he is mad. He watches the fog the way a "cat watches a mouse." Marlow interprets the natives' actions as protective and desperate, not aggressive or even defensive.

They travel through the thick fog until they come within a mile and a half below Kurtz's station. A bright green islet appears in the middle of the stream. Marlow can steer either left or right, with each path looking similar. He chooses the western passage because he had been informed the station was on the west side. It is narrower than he had anticipated. He steers the boat close to the bank, where the water is deepest. Marlow mentions the helmsman, a black man who thinks highly of himself. He wears a pair of brass earrings and blue cloth wrapper. When Marlow is next to him, this man steers with "no end of a swagger," but if no one is near he falls "prey to an abject funk." Marlow looks at the sounding-pole sticking further out of the water each time the poleman puts it in. This indicates how the water turns shallow.

The next moment, the poleman falls flat to the deck without the pole, and the fireman sits ducking by his furnace. Arrows fly. Marlow instructs the helmsman to steer straight. The pilgrims fire their guns into the jungle. Letting go of the steering, the helmsman grabs a gun. Marlow yells at him to return to his duty. He may have as well "ordered a tree not to sway in the wind." Instead, he steers the boat toward the bank. They hit overhanging bushes.

The helmsman holds his rifle and yells at the shore. Something big appears in the air, knocking the helmsman back. His head hits the wheel twice. He rolls back and stares up at Marlow, a shaft of spear sticking below his ribs. He lands at Marlow's feet. The helmsman's blood fills Marlow's shoes. The helmsman clutches the spear while Marlow forces himself to turn away from him and steer. He pulls the steam whistle cord repeatedly with one hand. The warlike yells die, the arrows stop.

Marlow and a pilgrim in pink pajamas stand over the helmsman. He dies without making a sound, a frown coming over his face at the last moment. Marlow tells the agent to steer. He tugs at his shoelaces. He believes Kurtz is dead now, too. Marlow throws one shoe overboard. He feels disappointment in not being able to speak with Kurtz now. Even though he had heard Kurtz was a swindler and thief, Marlow feels he is still a "gifted creature." Kurtz's ability to talk still fascinates him. He throws his other shoe overboard. Marlow thinks he has missed his destiny in life if he cannot hear Kurtz talk. He feels more lonely than if he had been "robbed of a belief."

On the *Nellie*, Marlow lights his pipe. The match shows his narrow face and dropped eyelids. He draws on his pipe, then the match goes out. This momentary switch in scene ends.

Marlow speaks of missing the privilege of listening to Kurtz. He amazes himself that he does not shed tears over missing Kurtz. He considers Kurtz "very little more than a voice." The "I" narrator cuts in again, telling us that Marlow becomes silent for a long time. We return quickly to Marlow's story. Marlow now jumps ahead in his story. He mentions women, specifically Kurtz's Intended, who will not appear until the end of the novella, after Marlow returns from Africa. He says she is "out of it," meaning out of touch with all that happened in Africa. He talks of Kurtz's baldness, an "ivory ball" of a head. Marlow marvels at the amount of ivory Kurtz had collected. It fills the mud shanty and the boat when they load it. There could not be a single tusk either above or below the ground. He says Kurtz watched over it and referred to everything as belonging to him.

Speaking philosophically, Marlow says Kurtz belonged to the "powers of darkness." He adds how Kurtz sat "amongst the devils of the land...." He tells about Kurtz's background, how he had been educated in England with a half-English mother and a half-French father. He says all "Europe contributed to the making of Kurtz." He finds out how Kurtz had been instructed by the International Society for the Suppression of Savage Customs to write a report.

Marlow sees it later, seventeen pages written before Kurtz's nerves "went wrong." A beautiful piece of writing, it described Kurtz presiding at midnight dances with unspeakable rites.

Marlow recalls Kurtz's words. In one section, Kurtz had written how the blacks approach the whites as if they possess the "might as of a deity...." He also had written "Exterminate all the brutes." Marlow considers the writing to be the "unbounded power of words." He tells how Kurtz believed his pamphlet would secure his future career. Kurtz was not common, Marlow says. His power to charm had influenced the natives, as well as himself. He cannot forget him, yet he is not sure it was worth the helmsman's death to reach him.

Marlow ends his jump ahead in the story, the "flash-forward." He returns to the helmsman's death. Marlow misses the helmsman and the partnership they had developed as they worked together. The bond now broken, he remembers the "profundity" of the helmsman's look before he had died. Marlow puts on dry slippers, then throws the helmsman's body overboard. The current takes his body, it rolls over twice, then disappears. Marlow says he had been a second-rate helmsman, but now he would be a first-class temptation—meaning food for the cannibals. Marlow steers after the funeral. Everyone on board believes Kurtz is dead. One red-haired pilgrim says they must have slaughtered everyone. Marlow says they at least had made a lot of smoke. He thinks they had missed their targets during the fight, by shooting too high. The screeching whistle had sent them running, he maintains. The manager talks of getting down the river for safety before it turns dark.

A decaying building with the jungle background fills the slope of a hill. They finally see the station. A white man wearing a hat like a cartwheel motions to them. Other human forms glide through the jungle. Marlow stops the engine and lets the boat drift. The manager tells the man about the attack. The man knows about it and says everything is all right. He reminds Marlow of a harlequin: bright clothes of blue, red, and yellow sparkling in the sun. He looks young with a boyish face, no beard, and little blue eyes. He asks Marlow if he is English, and Marlow answers with the same question. Pointing up the hill, he tells them Kurtz is there. Armed, the manager and pilgrims go to the house. The man comes aboard. He says the whistle will scare the natives, "simple people," he calls them. The sound of the whistle works better to drive the natives away than guns do, he says. People don't talk to Mr. Kurtz, he adds, they listen to him. The son of an arch-priest, he is Russian, had run away from school, and served on English ships. He had been wandering alone on the river for two years. He is twenty-five, not so young as he looks. He tells Marlow the small house, stack of wood, and note were his. Marlow hands him the book. He makes as if to kiss Marlow, but restrains himself. Marlow finds out that the notes in the book are in Russian, not cipher. He tells Marlow that the natives had attacked because they do not want Kurtz to be taken away, not to kill him and the crew. Kurtz has "enlarged" his mind, he adds. He opens his arms and stares at Marlow.

Analysis

Marlow hears second-hand information about Kurtz from the manager and his uncle. Their opinion of him contrasts Marlow's growing admiration for Kurtz. He gathers bits from them about Kurtz, the way we gather bits from him. He anticipates meeting Kurtz, mirroring our interest. Their fear of Kurtz and his success parallels Marlow's desire to meet him and draw his own conclusions. Marlow understands Kurtz's fine business sense when the manager talks of the ivory, "lots of it," coming from Kurtz's station. This period establishes Marlow's changing reason for his journey. At first, it was for the job and the adventure, but now Kurtz occupies his thoughts. He says he seemed "to see Kurtz for the first time." Surrounded by paddling savages, Kurtz leads the way "towards the depth of the wilderness." At this time, Marlow does not understand Kurtz's rejection of conventional society for unknown territory.

We come to see how the manager and his uncle represent the selfishness and greediness of civilized Europe. They care only about themselves, their positions, and promotions. They ridicule Kurtz's philosophy of how each station should be a "beacon on the road towards better things, a center for trade of course, but also for humanizing, improving, instructing." Kurtz's idyllic vision aggravates them. Ironically, we will find out how Kurtz's life and practices contrast with his once idealistic views. When the manager's uncle asks him if he feels well, we see the power of the jungle, as it weakens and kills people. The uncle gestures toward the forest as he suggests how the climate may destroy Kurtz. Marlow calls the man's wishes a "treacherous appeal to the lurking death, to the hidden evil, to the profound darkness of its heart." Physically, the jungle conquers most men, leaving only the strong to live on. The power of nature overwhelms the power of man.

Marlow then compares traveling farther into the jungle to prehistoric times. The "empty stream," "great silence," and "impenetrable forest" validate this association. No civilization or laws governed people then. Marlow recalls his own past "in the shape of an unrestful and noisy dream, remembered with wonder amongst the overwhelming realities of this strange world of plants, and water, and silence." As he journeys deeper into the forest, reality fades. A dream-like quality, with its "inner truth" surfaces. He adds to this idea of the ancient past without laws by speaking of the cannibals on the boat. These "fine fellows" show their progression to modern man by working well and not eating each other in front of Marlow. As civilized and tamed people, they fit Marlow's European view of man, not the native African, which he speaks of next. As the drums roll, Marlow sees the natives on shore. Their howling, leaping, and spinning thrill him. Their behavior evokes a "remote kinship with this wild and passionate roar." Instead of rejecting their outbursts, Marlow identifies with them; he understands that part in himself. Since the "mind of man is capable of anything," Marlow intellectually merges past and present.

This enables him to meet the truth before him—these savages dancing in the jungle. Notice how the farther he moves away from Europe, the more he identifies with the natives. The fireman, who fires the boiler, represents a combination of both worlds, savage and civilized. Marlow says he "ought to have been clapping his hands and stamping his feet on the bank." Physically, he resembles a typical native. He wears a charm made of rags around his arm and a piece of polished bone through his lower lip. He considers the fire in the boiler to be an "evil spirit." Since "he had been instructed," though, he works on the boat. He personifies the transformation from the savage native to the educated white man. Marlow compares him to a dog walking on his hind-legs, which simultaneously insults and compliments him.

The hut they come upon some fifty miles below the Inner Station foreshadows Marlow's meeting with the Russian and a packet of papers Kurtz will give him. We find out at the end of Section II of *Heart of Darkness* that the Russian had left the note, firewood, and book. Marlow handles the coverless book, *An Inquiry into some Points of Seamanship*, "with the greatest possible tenderness." A plain book, this work attracts Marlow because it represents "an honest concern for the right way of going to work." He appreciates the care necessary to write it. He compares having to stop reading to tearing himself "away from the shelter of an old and solid friendship." Later, in Section III, when Kurtz hands Marlow his personal papers, Marlow will handle them with extreme care, too. Their value transcends their tattered appearance.

As the boat progresses up the river, Marlow and the manager disagree about their navigation. The manager urges caution, while Marlow wants to push on. Fearing the warning alluded to in the Russian's note, the manager suggests traveling in daylight for safety. Yearning "to talk openly with Kurtz," Marlow intends to get there as quickly as possible. Any delay annoys him. He disregards the dangers.

Marlow returns to the idea of the savage cannibals. They belong to the beginnings of time and eat rotten hippo-meat. He marvels at how they simply do not overpower the white men to eat them. For all their supposed barbarity, the savages and cannibals control their behavior more than the white man, who initiates violence in the search for ivory and wealth. The cannibals' "primitive honor" restrains them from physical aggression. They even check their hunger through some kind of restricting code of law. The arguments between Marlow and the manager build the tension and accentuate their differences. Since Marlow thinks of Kurtz as "an enchanted princess sleeping in a fabulous castle," he wants to avoid caution and further delays. The closer Marlow gets to Kurtz, the more reckless he becomes. The manager always remains wary. Marlow's personal quest interferes with the manager's business-like approach. The forest turns thickest within a mile and a half of Kurtz's station. Trees stand in "serried ranks," twigs overhang the "current thickly," and a "broad strip of shadow" falls across the water.

Conrad intends this blurring on literal and symbolic levels. While the vegetation prevents Marlow from seeing the natives in the jungle, man's humanity and morality mix with his inhumanity and immorality. It becomes difficult to distinguish one from the other. The jungle disguises man's external and internal worlds. The densely matted forest allows the natives to attack Marlow's boat. Marlow sees "human limbs in movement" in the "tangled gloom," but cannot prepare for the arrows. The pilgrims, with their more sophisticated weapons, lose any advantage they might have. Accustomed to the jungle, the natives seize the initiative with their primitive spears. The pilgrims fire at random into the forest. They cannot see their targets, but their targets can see them. The helmsman's death in battle establishes Marlow's growing obsession with meeting Kurtz.

The helmsman suffers a horrible death, a spear hitting him in the side below the ribs. He spills a pool of blood onto the floor and Marlow's feet. After watching him die, Marlow thinks that Kurtz must be dead as well. "For the moment that was the dominant thought," he adds, showing his disregard for the helmsman's life. This man means little to him in relation to Kurtz. Later, he checks himself by saying that meeting Kurtz may not have been "exactly worth the life we lost in getting to him." When Marlow next considers Kurtz to "present himself as a voice," we see how Conrad connects him to Kurtz. In Section I, the narrator had said Marlow telling his story "had been no more to us than a voice." The way we listen to Marlow parallels the way Marlow listens to Kurtz. Marlow believes Kurtz to be "something altogether without substance." This is what Marlow is for us, the reader—merely a voice speaking words. Of course, Conrad throws in a catch. There is "substance" to Kurtz's story and Marlow's story. Marlow must interpret Kurtz's words, while we must interpret Marlow's words. These comparisons determine important distinctions. Marlow is like Kurtz because he leads, but he also resembles us because he listens.

Next, Conrad interrupts Marlow's story to return to the *Nellie*. These transitions accomplish two things: one, they force us to listen more intently; two, they break the dream-like quality of

Marlow's journey by bringing us back to the reality of the present on the boat. The first time, Marlow lights his pipe, which illuminates his face momentarily. The second time, Marlow becomes silent. The idea of light and dark couples with sound and silence. The alternating shades of white and black suggest the good and evil of the actions of Marlow's company toward the natives, the changing shades in the jungle, and the white Europeans and the black Africans. The sound and silence reflect the intermittent noises in the jungle, and Kurtz's voice in life against his silence in death for Marlow.

Marlow then jumps forward in his narrative. By breaking the chronological structure, Conrad again forces us to listen to Marlow's suggestion of looking beneath the surface to understand the finer points of his tale. We cannot simply accept the story as told, but must consider how Conrad gives us information. The deception Conrad incorporates in his narrative mirrors the deception Marlow encounters in the jungle. While he navigates the Congo, we navigate his story.

One oversight affects the rest of the journey/story. In his jump ahead, Marlow offers us glimpses of Kurtz before he appears. First, he mentions Kurtz's Intended, the woman who waits for him in Europe. She will not appear until the end of the novella. He covets ivory, with his bald head even summoning the image of "an ivory ball." He refers to everything as "my," and belongs to the powers of darkness. Kurtz represents evil, a connection to man's dark side. In a "high seat amongst the devils of the land," Kurtz leads the natives in literal and symbolic ways. Marlow's ambition of speaking to Kurtz shows how he wants to embrace and understand Kurtz, his world, and his philosophy. In a sense, Marlow wants to transform himself into one of the natives, a follower of this mad deity. Marlow attributes Kurtz's origin not to Africa and the jungle, but Europe. Since "all Europe contributed to the making of Kurtz," we see how Conrad rejects the idea of the black natives as evil, instead accusing the white European society of creating this devilish man. Here, Conrad flips the traditional image of white/good and black/bad around. Appearances can be deceiving, as the jungle often proves. Kurtz's report for the International Society for the Suppression of Savage Customs enhances his relationship to the dark side. Marlow learns of the "unspeakable rites" Kurtz presided at, the sacrifices "offered up to him," and the "exterminate all the brutes" ideology he espoused. Kurtz preaches a racial inequality, with the blacks looking at the whites "in the nature of supernatural beings." Ironically, Kurtz becomes a savage while reporting for their suppression. Marlow does not say whether he approves of Kurtz's ideas, even if he admires the "unbounded power of eloquence" of the words. Confused by the contradicting images of Kurtz, Marlow thinks that "whatever he was, he was not common." He could "charm or frighten rudimentary souls."

In Section I, the narrator said "Marlow was not typical." Conrad develops another similarity, here, suggesting how Marlow charms us with his words, and frightens us with them, as well. Marlow says Kurtz will not be forgotten, which he will assure because "as it turned out, he was to have the care of his memory." Will we carry on Marlow's memory?

The appearance of the Russian next adds a sort of strange, humorous element to the story. A brightly dressed "harlequin" with blue, red, and yellow patches over all his clothes, this man announces Kurtz's presence to Marlow. He is reminiscent of the "Fool" in Shakespeare's *King Lear*, a character who looks nonsensical, yet imparts much wisdom. He speaks to Marlow while the manager and pilgrims investigate Kurtz's situation. He fills in some missing details for Marlow. He tells him that the hut, firewood, and note had been his. He explains how the natives had run for fear from the boat's whistle, adding how they "don't want him to go"—meaning Kurtz. And, most importantly for Marlow, he relates how Kurtz's speaking had captivated him. Almost as a sign of thanks for these bits of information, Marlow gives him the book he had found in the hut. The Russian returns the thanks by making to kiss Marlow, but "restrained himself." This act foreshadows Marlow's return of Kurtz's manuscript to Kurtz's Intended at the end of the novella. Marlow always handles with care the things he treasures, particularly Kurtz's memory. The Russian says Kurtz has "enlarged" his mind. Kurtz's life has answered some deep need for the Russian. Marlow's need to meet Kurtz will be answered shortly, in the next section. For the moment, though, when the Russian "opened his arms wide," Marlow receives his long-awaited invitation to Kurtz's world. This last image alludes to a religious service, where a priest (the Russian) invites his parishioner (Marlow) to worship their god (Kurtz).

Study Questions

1. When he is on the boat, who does Marlow overhear speaking about Kurtz?

2. Why does Marlow compare the jungle to prehistoric times?

3. How does the cannibals' food affect Marlow?

4. Why does the book Marlow finds in the hut interest him?

5. Why couldn't the men aboard the boat spend their money for food?

6. Who aboard the boat is killed during the attack?

7. How does Marlow scare the natives during the fight?

8. Why does Marlow throw his shoes overboard?

9. Why does the Russian leave a note on the woodpile?

10. Why did Kurtz write a report?

Answers

1. Marlow overhears the manager and his uncle talk of Kurtz.

2. The violence, degradation, and lack of civility in the jungle remind Marlow of prehistoric times.

3. The cannibals' hippo-meat is rotten, smells, and makes Marlow think of his own hunger.

4. The book in the hut interests Marlow because it reflects a task planned and done well.

5. The men on the boat could not buy food because the manager did not stop, and/or the villages were destroyed.

6. The helmsman dies during the attack.

7. Marlow blows the steam whistle and the natives fear the noise.

8. Marlow throws his shoes overboard because they are soaked with blood from the helmsman's wounds.

9. The Russian leaves a note to tell someone to hurry and prepare for the coming danger.

10. Kurtz writes a document because he was instructed to chronicle his experience with the savages.

Suggested Essay Topics

1. Marlow hears about Kurtz when other people talk about him. The accountant, brickmaker, manager, and the manager's uncle speak of Kurtz to each other and/or Marlow. He pieces together their offhand remarks to form his opinion of Kurtz. From their references, characterize Kurtz. Is he admirable, a good ivory-agent, successful? Is it possible their positions influence their feelings toward Kurtz?

2. Marlow's journey to Africa enables him to meet for the first time the natives, people unlike him in many ways. How does Marlow, as well as the other white men, contrast with the blacks? Focus not only on their physical differences, but their behavior and general way of life. Are they representative of their distinct cultures, since one group comes from "civilized" Europe and the other comes from the "dark" continent?

3. A few times during Section I, Marlow mentions how he anticipates meeting Kurtz. Why does Kurtz intrigue him? Has the gossip about Kurtz fueled his interest? Is there any logical reason why he becomes obsessed with meeting Kurtz, a white man like himself?

4. The conversation between Marlow and the manager in Section I, and the talk between the manager and his uncle at the beginning of Section II, establish the manager's character. According to Marlow, he has no good qualities. Show how the manager is greedy, self-centered, and more of a hindrance to Marlow than a help. Remember, the manager envies Kurtz, a man Marlow longs to meet. Could this account for Marlow's unflattering picture of him?

5. Conrad ends Section I between when the manager's uncle arrives and the manager talks to his uncle about Kurtz. Section II ends right after the Russian greets Marlow and tells them preliminary information about himself and Kurtz. Why does Conrad end these sections here? Are they important breaks in the plot? Would *Heart of Darkness* have been different if Conrad had left the novella as one chapter, with no separate sections?

SECTION FOUR

Heart of Darkness

Section III (pages 50–72)

New Characters:

Kurtz's Black Mistress: *black woman in the jungle who wears many ornaments*

A Clean-Shaved Man, Kurtz's "Cousin," a Journalist: *three people who visit Marlow in Europe to get Kurtz's papers*

Kurtz's Intended: *Kurtz's fiancée in Europe*

Summary

Marlow looks at the Russian, whose "improbable, inexplicable, and altogether bewildering" existence fascinates him. He wonders how he had survived in the jungle. Marlow imagines he will disappear before his eyes. The Russian tells Marlow to take Kurtz away quickly. Marlow does not envy the Russian's devotion to Kurtz because he had not "meditated over it." He believes it is a "most dangerous thing."

Marlow compares the Russian and Kurtz to ships "becalmed near each other." The Russian fulfills Kurtz's need to have an audience. He says he had talked to Kurtz many nights, especially about love. Kurtz had made him "see" things.

The Russian throws his arms up in praise of Kurtz. The headman of Marlow's wood-cutters looks at Marlow. Frightened, for the first time he sees the jungle as a dark place without hope.

The Russian's friendship with Kurtz had been broken, not continuous. He had nursed Kurtz through two illnesses. Often, he had waited many days for Kurtz to return from his wanderings.

He tells Marlow how Kurtz had discovered villages, a lake, and searched for ivory. It had always been worth the wait. Marlow reminds the Russian how Kurtz had run out of goods to trade for ivory. The Russian says, "There's a good lot of cartridges left even yet."

Marlow figures that Kurtz had raided the country. He asks if Kurtz had the natives following him. The Russian says the natives adore Kurtz, lured by his "thunder and lightning." He says Kurtz can be terrible at times, but no one can judge him as you would an ordinary man. Once, Kurtz had tried to kill him, he says. Kurtz had wanted his ivory. The Russian had given it to him. He had to be careful, until he had reestablished his friendship with Kurtz. He had nursed him through his second illness then. Marlow says Kurtz is mad. The Russian objects. He tells Marlow he will change his mind when he hears Kurtz speak.

Marlow sees people moving in the forest through his binoculars. He compares the woods to the "closed door of a prison." The silence disturbs him. The Russian tells Marlow that Kurtz is very ill now. Only lately had he come to the river, after an absence of many months. Marlow sees round knobs on posts near Kurtz's house. They are "black, dried, sunken" heads. The first one in the row faces him. It seems to smile at some "dream of that eternal slumber." Marlow believes the heads show Kurtz's lack of restraint. The wilderness had made him mad, he figures. Marlow can only wonder if Kurtz knows of his own "deficiency." He puts down his binoculars.

The Russian tells Marlow about Kurtz's ascendancy, how the chiefs venerate him, and how keeping him alive has occupied all his time. Marlow does not want to hear about the ceremonies used to honor Kurtz. Marlow believes he is in a "region of subtle horrors." The Russian justifies Kurtz's savagery by telling Marlow the heads had belonged to rebels, Kurtz's opposition. Kurtz's trying life, he adds, had led him to these cruel acts. Only keeping Kurtz alive, the Russian says he had nothing to do with these killings.

A group of men carrying Kurtz on a stretcher, appears from around the house. Waist-deep in the grass, they appear to rise from the ground. Naked human beings with spears, bows, and shields follow. The bushes shake and the grass sways, but then stop in "attentive immobility," as if everything waits for something to happen next. The Russian tells Marlow that if Kurtz does not say the right thing, they are done for.

Kurtz sits up. Marlow resents the absurd danger. Through his glasses, he sees Kurtz move his arm, talk, and nod his head. He realizes Kurtz means "short" in German, and feels the name fits, though he looks "at least seven feet long." The cage of his ribs and bones of his arms show. He thinks of Kurtz as an "animated image of death." Marlow hears Kurtz's deep voice from afar.

Kurtz falls back, then the savages carry him forward again. Some savages vanish into the forest, which after breathing them out, was drawing them back in.

Some pilgrims carry Kurtz's guns as they walk behind the stretcher. Bent over and talking, the manager walks beside him. They take Kurtz aboard the steamer and put him in a little cabin. Kurtz plays with the letters they had brought him. Marlow notices both the fire in Kurtz's eyes and the dullness. Speaking for the first time, he says to Marlow, "I am glad." Kurtz had received special recommendations about Marlow. The grave voice contains power. The manager appears in the doorway and the Russian stares at the shore. Marlow follows his glance.

A woman appears along the shore. She wears brass leggings to the knee, brass wire gauntlets to the elbow, and necklaces of glass beads. A "wild and gorgeous apparition of a woman," she walks with measured steps. She wears the "value of several elephant tusks upon her." The land, wilderness, and mysterious life seem to look at her. She approaches the steamer. Standing still, she faces them. The Russian growls, and the pilgrims murmur at Marlow's back. She lifts up her arms, the shadows darting out. Silence hangs over the scene. She turns and walks away, looking back at the men once.

The Russian says he would have shot her if she had tried to come aboard. He had been keeping her away from Kurtz for two weeks. According to the Russian, she had created problems. Once, while pointing at the Russian, she had to talk to Kurtz for an hour. Kurtz had been ill that day, or else "there would have been mischief." Marlow hears Kurtz yelling at the manager. He accuses him of caring only for the ivory. He says he is not as sick as the manager believes he is. The manager has interfered with his plans, and he will return to complete them. The manager walks from behind the curtain and tells Marlow how "low" Kurtz is, how he has done more harm than good for the company, and how they have done all they can for him. He agrees there is much ivory, but on the whole "the trade will suffer." Despite Kurtz's amazing success in obtaining ivory, the manager considers his method "unsound." Marlow ignores the manager's disapproval. He tells him that Kurtz is a remarkable man. The manager says Kurtz "was" a remarkable man. According to the manager, Marlow belongs to the same group as Kurtz.

Kurtz is "as good as buried," Marlow believes. The Russian taps Marlow on the shoulder and stammers out broken sentences. Marlow implores the Russian to speak. The Russian believes the white men hold ill-will toward him. Marlow agrees, saying the manager wants him hanged. The Russian plans to leave the area for a military post three hundred miles away. He asks Marlow to keep secrets so as to save Kurtz's reputation. Marlow promises.

He tells Marlow that Kurtz had ordered the attack to prevent them from taking him away. He is a simple man, though, and does not understand these matters. He has a canoe and three black fellows waiting for him. He asks for cartridges. Marlow hands them to him. The Russian takes some of Marlow's good English tobacco. He asks Marlow for shoes, showing him soles tied like sandals under his bare feet. Marlow gives him an old pair. He tells Marlow how Kurtz had read his own poetry, and he will never again meet a man like him. He rolls his eyes with delight and repeats how Kurtz had enlarged his mind. With cartridges in one pocket and the seamanship book in the other, the Russian vanishes. Marlow compares him to a "phenomenon!"

Marlow wakes after midnight. A fire burns on the hill, a line of agents guards the ivory, and men chant to themselves. Where Kurtz's "adorers" keep a vigil, red gleams waver in the forest against the intense blackness. Marlow dozes off again. When he wakes, he looks into the cabin and sees a light, but not Kurtz. An agent sleeps on a deck chair three feet from Marlow. Leaping ashore, Marlow says he will never betray Kurtz. He feels "jealous of sharing with any one the peculiar blackness of that experience."

Marlow discovers a trail in the wet grass. Kurtz crawls on all-fours. Marlow surprises himself by thinking of one of the knitting women. He believes he will never make it back to the steamer, instead living alone in the woods to an old age. He confuses the beat of the drums with that of his heart. He overcomes Kurtz, some thirty feet from a fire. Kurtz stands "like a vapor exhaled by the earth." He fears Kurtz will shout. A sorcerer, or witch-man, stands close behind them. Kurtz tells Marlow, "Go away—hide yourself." When Marlow asks Kurtz if he knows what he is doing, he says, "Perfectly."

Marlow threatens to smash Kurtz's head, even though nothing is near to use. Kurtz says his plans have been thwarted and he "was on the threshold of great things." Marlow assures him of success in Europe. He believes Kurtz belongs to no one, "nobody either above or below." His common words suggest dreams and nightmares. Kurtz's "perfectly clear" intelligence appears before Marlow. He says Kurtz's mad soul defies description. Marlow carries him back to the couch, comparing Kurtz's weight to a child's. He shakes, though, as if he "had carried half a ton on my back down that hill."

At noon the next day, with Kurtz aboard, Marlow steers the steamer away. Covered in dirt from head to foot, three men strut on the slope. Blacks fill the clearing, the black woman among them. They nod their horned heads, sway their bodies, and shake black feathers toward the river. The black woman puts out her hands and shouts. In chorus, the mob responds to her sounds, reminiscent of a "satanic litany."

In the pilot-house, Marlow asks Kurtz if he understands their actions. Kurtz answers, "Do I not?" Pulling the string of the whistle, Marlow scares the natives away. The pilgrims get their rifles. Someone on deck tells him to stop. The three men fall face down on the shore. Only the black woman remains in view. She stretches her arms after them over the river. The men aboard the boat begin firing, the smoke blocking Marlow's vision.

The steamer heads toward the sea at twice the speed it had come up the river. The manager watches Kurtz and Marlow. Kurtz is dying. The pilgrims look at Marlow with disfavor. He considers himself numbered with the dead. He accepts this "unforeseen partnership."

Kurtz mutters of his Intended, station, career, and ideas. He speaks of wanting kings to meet him at railway stations, a childish concept to Marlow. He insists on having the "right motives." He asks Marlow to close the shutters, and Marlow obliges.

The steamer breaks down, as Marlow had expected. One morning, Kurtz hands him papers and a photograph tied with a shoe-string. He tells Marlow to keep them in his care, away from the manager, the "noxious fool." Kurtz mutters, "Live rightly, die, die...." Marlow believes he is rehearsing for some speech, or repeating a newspaper article.

Marlow spends more time helping the engine-driver fix the boat than speaking to Kurtz. One night, Kurtz says he is waiting for death. Marlow says, "Oh, nonsense." Marlow has never seen anything like the changes on Kurtz's face as he approached death. Kurtz's last words are, "The horror! The horror!"

Marlow goes to the mess-room and sits opposite the manager. He avoids his glance. Flies stream over the lamp, cloth, hands, and faces. The manager's boy peeks in the doorway, and says, "Mistah Kurtz—he dead." The pilgrims run to see, but Marlow stays to eat dinner. The voice is gone. The next day they bury Kurtz in a muddy hole. "And then they very nearly buried me," Marlow adds.

Marlow cannot compare himself to Kurtz, he says, because Kurtz had something to say. "The horror" is an expression of belief, a "moral victory paid for by innumerable defeats," he reasons. Kurtz had been able to summarize and judge with his final pronouncement. He remains loyal to Kurtz because of this conviction. Marlow returns to Europe, back to the "sepulchral city." He resents the sight of people hurrying about, drinking beer, and eating. He feels they do not know what he now knows. He often runs a fever and "was not very well at the time." His aunt tries to nurse him. He hears of Kurtz's mother's death, watched over by his Intended.

One day a company official stops by to get Kurtz's writings. Marlow says he had two fights about them with the manager, and he still refuses to give them up. The man says the company needs the reports, adding how it would be a great loss if he could not get the papers. Marlow finally gives him the "Suppression of Savage Customs" with the postscript torn off. He wants more. "Expect nothing else," Marlow says.

Two days later, another man, calling himself Kurtz's "cousin," appears. He is an organist and tells Marlow that Kurtz had been a talented musician. Marlow does not doubt this man's opinion. Marlow adds how to this day he does not know what Kurtz's profession was. He had been a painter, a journalist, a "universal genius." Marlow gives him some family letters and unimportant memoranda.

Then a journalist shows up. He considers Kurtz to have been a politician, an extremist leader. He says Kurtz could not write, but "heavens! how that man could talk." The man says Kurtz's faith could make himself believe anything. Marlow hands him the report, the man saying he will publish it. Left with a packet of letters and a portrait of a beautiful girl, he wants to visit Kurtz's Intended.

Kurtz's soul, body, station, plans, ivory, and career had passed out of Marlow's hands by now. Only his memory and this woman survive. He recalls one day when Kurtz had complained how the company would try to claim the ivory as theirs, though he had collected it himself. At her house, Marlow has a vision of Kurtz on a stretcher, as he whispers again "The horror! The horror!"

All in black, she comes forward in her drawing room. It is more than a year after Kurtz's death. She mourns for him, as if he had died "only yesterday." Marlow hands her the packet. When she asks Marlow if he had known Kurtz well, he says, "I knew him as well as it is possible for one man to know another." She had not been able to share her memories of Kurtz with anyone since his mother's death. Marlow says he had heard how her family had disapproved of the engagement.

They promise always to remember him. She says he will live on because of his words and because "his goodness shone in every act." She puts out her arms across the light of the window. This action reminds Marlow of the black woman's movements in the jungle. She regrets not being with Kurtz at his death. Marlow says he had stayed with him until the end.

When she asks about Kurtz's last words, Marlow says they were her name. She sighs, saying, "I knew it—I was sure!" Marlow believes he could not have told the truth, something too painful for her to bear. She hides her face in her hands and weeps. Marlow expects the house to collapse for telling a lie, but "the heavens do not fall for such a trifle."

We return to the *Nellie*, with Marlow in the pose of a meditating Buddha. The story is over. The Director says they have lost the first of the ebb. The narrator raises his head and sees a black bank of clouds, the tranquil Thames, and an overcast sky. All "lead into the heart of an immense darkness." The novella ends as it had begun, in darkness.

Analysis

Section III opens with the Russian extolling his admiration for Kurtz, his idol. "Something like admiration—like envy" for the Russian, Marlow listens to Kurtz's exploits—how he talks eloquently, discovers ivory and land, and receives adoration from natives.

The Russian never says anything derogatory or negative about Kurtz, even though Kurtz had tried to kill him over some ivory.

While Marlow by this time admires Kurtz, he rejects the Russian's complete devotion. Since the Russian "had not meditated over it," Marlow figures it to border on a "most dangerous thing."

The Russian embraces Kurtz "with a sort of eager fatalism." Marlow still judges him objectively. Considering Kurtz "mad," Marlow contrasts the Russian's unwavering idolization. This insight into Kurtz's behavior tempers Marlow's growing reverence. We also discover how Kurtz has suffered two illnesses, the nature of which we are not told.

By the next scene, however, when Marlow sees the heads attached to poles, we know that Kurtz suffers from mental illness. Marlow considers them "not ornamental but symbolic." "Food for thought," they show Kurtz's extreme policies. His actions exceed acceptable behavior. They show no "restraint in the gratification of his lusts." Not coincidentally, only one head faces Marlow, the rest pointing the other way. As a symbol, this represents Kurtz staring at Marlow, or Marlow coming to terms with his other half, the side similar to Kurtz, where desires dominate logic.

Marlow attributes Kurtz's madness to the jungle. By taking a "terrible vengeance" out on him, it has forced Kurtz to abandon morality and reasonable judgment. The whispering forest echoes "loudly within" Kurtz because he is "hollow at the core...." This shatters Marlow's earlier image of Kurtz.

At this point, Marlow compares Kurtz's world to a "region of subtle horrors." He denounces Kurtz, considering him "no idol of mine." The Russian opposes Marlow's refutation by justifying Kurtz's savagery. Since the heads belonged to rebels, Kurtz had no choice. Marlow rejects the Russian's explanation. A few moments later, Kurtz appears for the first time. Marlow sees him "in the gloom," while he stands "in the sunshine." This contrast of light and dark shows how Marlow still isolates himself from Kurtz's world. The natives trail behind, though, as if they follow a god.

When Marlow notices Kurtz's deep voice, he completes the idea he had established earlier—Kurtz as more of a spiritual being than a physical one. Kurtz's "thin arm," "bony head," and eyes of an "apparition" de-emphasize his physicality. Marlow thinks of him as "an animated image of death carved out of old ivory."

On the boat, Kurtz's first words to Marlow, "I am glad," represent an ironic acknowledgment. Since people had mentioned Marlow to Kurtz, they show the simple pleasure of meeting someone. However, we know Marlow feels the same way toward Kurtz, even with his recent doubtings. Marlow could have spoken these words, in turn.

Kurtz's black mistress, "the wild and gorgeous apparition of a woman," links him to a woman in Africa the way his Intended connects him to a woman in Europe. Although the pilgrims and the Russian disapprove of her, she stands immune from their censure. She is a reverse Kurtz in a female form, though more of a physical presence with her "flash of barbarous ornaments." She never speaks, whereas Kurtz is a voice. Her "savage and superb" physical strength opposes Kurtz's physical frailty.

The manager questions Kurtz's sanity by calling his methods "unsound." He believes he lacks judgment. Marlow defends Kurtz, saying, "Nevertheless, I think Mr. Kurtz is a remarkable man." Marlow sides with Kurtz for two reasons. First, he dislikes the manager, so this contradiction, he knows, annoys him. Second, when he finds himself "lumped along with Kurtz," he takes it as a compliment.

This affinity determines the next scene, when Marlow promises the Russian that he will save Kurtz's reputation by keeping his savagery secret. Marlow surprises himself. "I did not know how truly I spoke," he says. When the Russian flees the area, we see a further connection with Marlow. The Russian has a "canoe and three black fellows waiting" to take him away. This parallels Marlow's steamer and crew on a smaller level. The Russian also needs shoes, which Marlow gives him. Remember earlier, Marlow needed shoes when the helmsman's blood had soaked into them. The Russian also says he will never meet such a man again. We know Marlow feels the same way.

The next scene turns dream-like. Marlow falls asleep, then awakes after midnight with fires burning and drums filling the air "with muffled shocks and a lingering vibration." The natives keep "their uneasy vigil" over Kurtz's house, a religious connotation. When Marlow chases Kurtz through the jungle to get him back to the boat, we notice how possessive of him he feels. He says he is "jealous of sharing with any one the peculiar blackness of that experience." Yet, he shares the memory of Kurtz with us as he narrates his adventure.

Kurtz's crawling on all-fours to escape links him to the native in Section I who had crawled on all-fours to drink from the river. They both crawl to survive, they both are near death, and they both fall victim to the jungle. And, since the natives worship Kurtz, they should share similarities.

In the fragmented conversation with Kurtz, Marlow fluctuates between wanting to kill Kurtz and assuring him of success in Europe based on his accomplishments. Marlow knows that Kurtz personifies contradictions. There is nothing "above or below him"; he is mad, yet intelligent; and, he is "alone in the wilderness," yet Marlow "supported him, his long bony arm clasped round my neck." During the next scene, the natives and black mistress line the jungle to watch Kurtz leave, their god being taken from them. She leads them in a "roaring chorus," suggesting a religious response at a formal service. When Marlow asks Kurtz if he understands their actions, he smiles and says, "Do I not?" He understands their devotion, and how removing him betrays their belief.

Marlow then scares the natives, to the dismay of some people on the boat. He fears for his life, so he blows the whistle. Only the black mistress remains, her arms "stretched tragically" in the pose of a priestess. She stays devoted until the end, the same way Kurtz's Intended, another woman, will at the end.

As they escape "out of the heart of darkness," Marlow continues his dedication to Kurtz. The manager and pilgrims look upon him with "disfavor." His "unforeseen partnership" with Kurtz forges his complicity. Marlow even helps Kurtz by closing the shutters to the outside, as he requests. Kurtz's separation from the jungle unnerves him. He does not want to leave Africa and his followers the same way Marlow does not want to leave Kurtz. This explains why Marlow murmurs "Oh, nonsense" when Kurtz says he waits for death. "The horror! The horror!"—Kurtz's last words—suggest many interpretations. They refer to his death, his destroyed plans, his submission to his evil side, and the pain of life. Marlow "blew the candle out" and then left the cabin. This extinguished light signifies not only Kurtz's life, but the sanctity he embodies for Marlow.

Appropriately, a native announces Kurtz's death. Marlow would not because he would rather deny it. Since Kurtz represents a god, his followers should pronounce his death. Ironically, Marlow appears "brutally callous" by not remaining with Kurtz, we know, this is not true. His emotional closeness to Kurtz surpasses any pilgrim's. Marlow agrees with the Russian when he proclaims Kurtz's greatness. Kurtz "had something to say." His judgment, as summarized in "The Horror!" expresses conviction and an "appalling face of a glimpsed truth." Kurtz's life extended to extremes. He "stepped over the edge," while Marlow "had been permitted to draw back his hesitating foot." Marlow withdraws where Kurtz advances.

This distinction represents the Freudian psychological terms ego and id. The id is man's instinctual impulses and the satisfaction of primal needs. This is Kurtz, the man who satisfies his needs by returning to the primitive forest. He lets loose his urges, no matter how excessive or deviant they are. Conversely, Marlow is the ego—the part of the personality that controls behavior and external reality. He questions the savagery, killing, and abandonment of laws for pleasure.

Marlow never relinquishes his rational side for Kurtz's irrational one. Marlow is the way Kurtz once was, and Kurtz is what Marlow does not want to be. When Marlow returns to Europe, the daily routine of working, eating, and drinking bores him. His experience has taught him things these people can never know. He feels like "laughing in their faces so full of stupid importance."

He runs a fever, fulfilling the doctor's predictions in Section I, when he had said that the changes take place inside. Like Kurtz, Marlow is mentally, not physically, ill. His "inexcusable behavior" proves the jungle's influence.

The visits by the company official, Kurtz's "cousin," and the journalist illustrate their impersonal concern for Kurtz's life, unlike Marlow's deeply personal one. They want his papers for official and public reasons. Marlow gives them only unimportant papers, saving the personal letters and photographs for Kurtz's Intended. Marlow finds the seamanship book and Kurtz's writings. He gives the book to the Russian because he knows he values it, and Kurtz's letters to his Intended because she values them.

Marlow's last act—his visit to Kurtz's Intended more than a year after his death—completes Marlow's journey. She constitutes the European version of Kurtz's black mistress in Africa. Her "fair hair," "pale visage," and "pure brow" oppose the black woman's ornamental excesses. She speaks of her loss to Marlow. The black woman had expressed it through physical movements. They talk of intimacy, knowing Kurtz, and love. Ironically, she says she "knew him best." In many ways, Marlow knows Kurtz on a deeper level than she does. She also is unaware of his black mistress, barbaric actions, and mental illness. She says he "drew men towards him." For Marlow, nothing could be more true. Mesmerized by Kurtz, he remains loyal to his memory. Marlow avoids breaking the "illusion that shone with an unearthly glow" in Kurtz's Intended. He believes she is not capable of dealing with the truth, a force too powerful to oppose. Her misconception shows when she says Kurtz's "goodness shone in every act." Marlow agrees, furthering the deception. He connects Kurtz's Intended to the black mistress. These women show their love for Kurtz by cherishing their image of him—each mirroring their culture's ways.

Let's return for a moment to the oil painting Marlow had seen in Section I. We now recognize a reference to the black mistress and his Intended in the picture. The blindfold and torch reflect his Intended, her delusion toward Kurtz and her light of love in his dark world. The somber, black background and stately movement reflect his black mistress, the African jungle and her measured gestures. With only Kurtz's words left to them, Marlow and the woman talk of his verbal gifts. When she wants to know Kurtz's last words, Marlow lies and tells her they had been her name, not "The horror! The horror!"

Earlier, in Section I, Kurtz had said he detested a lie because there is a "taint of death" in it. He lies to Kurtz's Intended to shield her from the truth. He has seen the truth in the jungle, but knows the lie here is better. Kurtz's Intended cries, and, in so doing, comforts herself. It would have been "too dark altogether" for her. Marlow finalizes his idea of "how out of touch with truth women are," which he had announced in Section II. He also atones, in a way, for his attitude toward his aunt for helping him secure his job. There he had belittled a woman, here he protects a woman.

The framed narrative ends. We return to the *Nellie* and Marlow's "pose of a meditating Buddha." As we had asked in Section I, what has he learned and suffered? Now we can answer these questions. He has learned of man's darker side, his attraction toward evil, through Kurtz. He has discovered how the heart of darkness is not only a physical place (Africa), but a place within all men. He has suffered from seeing that darker side. Few people can claim this, which explains why Marlow "sat apart," from the others on the boat. Finally, the Director says, "We have lost the first of the ebb." He ignores Marlow's tale. Nothing reaches him, none of the philosophy and insights into human nature. The narrator lifts his head and sees "the heart of an immense darkness" in the distance. Marlow's story has enlightened him. If we have listened, it has done the same for us.

Study Questions

1. Why does the Russian nurse Kurtz through two illnesses?

2. What frightening sight does Marlow see outside Kurtz's house?

3. Who is with Kurtz when Marlow first sees him?

4. Why does the manager disapprove of Kurtz?

5. Why does the Russian leave Kurtz's area?

6. Why is Kurtz carried from the forest?

7. Why does Kurtz give Marlow papers before he dies?

8. Explain the irony of where they bury Kurtz.

9. Why do three people visit Marlow when he returns to Europe?

10. What lie does Marlow tell Kurtz's Intended?

Answers

1. The Russian's admiration and love for Kurtz compels him to nurse Kurtz through two illnesses.

2. Marlow sees heads stuck on poles outside Kurtz's house.

3. Weak, Kurtz is on a stretcher carried by the natives when Marlow first sees him.

4. The manager disapproves of Kurtz because he believes Kurtz has done more harm than good for the company by his unsound methods.

5. The Russian leaves Kurtz's area because he fears the manager wants him killed.

6. Kurtz is taken from the forest to a cabin on the boat so he can be rescued and cured.

7. Kurtz gives Marlow a packet of letters to preserve his work and memory.

8. Worshipped in life by the natives, Kurtz is buried in a "muddy hole," a place of filth and emptiness.

9. Three people visit Marlow in Europe to get Kurtz's writings.

10. He tells her Kurtz's last words were her name.

Suggested Essay Topics

1. From what the Russian says, he worships Kurtz. He always praises him, even justifying Kurtz's barbaric killings. Marlow admires Kurtz also. How, though, does their admiration for Kurtz differ? Is the Russian's more exaggerated, and Marlow's

more controlled? Since the Russian already knows Kurtz and has spoken to him, and Marlow has not met Kurtz yet, can that influence their respective feelings?

2. There are many indications of Kurtz's mental illness. The decapitated heads on poles outside his home, his "exterminate all the brutes" philosophy, and his obsessive quest for ivory show his "unsound method," as the manager terms it. Is Kurtz mad, or has he simply adapted to a barbaric society? Is he just playing by the rules of the jungle, which differ from those of a civilized society?

3. Though seemingly minor, the three women are important to Marlow's adventure. His aunt, Kurtz's black mistress, and Kurtz's Intended influence the story in various ways. Compare the three of them. What does each one represent? Include how they come from different parts of society with separate values and beliefs, especially Kurtz's two loves.

4. Kurtz appears in *Heart of Darkness* for a very short time. He does and says little. Why then is he so important to the story? Why didn't Conrad expand his actual role? Does his limited appearance detract from his importance?

5. Describe the three people who visit Marlow to get Kurtz's papers after he returns to Europe from Africa. What do their positions and interest in Kurtz say about Kurtz's reputation? Why is Marlow so reluctant about giving them Kurtz's papers? What are his personal reasons for protecting them?

6. Besides Marlow and Kurtz, Conrad identifies all the characters who appear by description, not name. We see the chief accountant, the manager, the manager's uncle, the helmsman, the Russian, etc. Why does Conrad use these vague references? By not giving them names, does he shift the emphasis away from them, even though they all contribute to Marlow's journey? Is their function, as suggested through their title, more important than their name?

SECTION FIVE

Bibliography

Conrad, Joseph. *Heart of Darkness and The Secret Sharer*. New York: Bantam Books, 1981.

Conrad, Joseph. *The Nigger of the Narcissus*. New York: Dell Publishing Company, Incorporated, 1960.

Gurko, Leo. *Joseph Conrad: Giant in Exile.* New York: The Macmillan Company, 1962.

Karl, Frederick R., and Magalaner, Marvin. *A Reader's Guide to Twentieth-Century English Novels, New York: Octagon Books, 1984.*

DOVER · THRIFT · EDITIONS

FICTION

ADVENTURES OF HUCKLEBERRY FINN, Mark Twain. (0-486-28061-6)

THE AWAKENING, Kate Chopin. (0-486-27786-0)

A CHRISTMAS CAROL, Charles Dickens. (0-486-26865-9)

FRANKENSTEIN, Mary Shelley. (0-486-28211-2)

HEART OF DARKNESS, Joseph Conrad. (0-486-26464-5)

PRIDE AND PREJUDICE, Jane Austen. (0-486-28473-5)

THE SCARLET LETTER, Nathaniel Hawthorne. (0-486-28048-9)

THE ADVENTURES OF TOM SAWYER, Mark Twain. (0-486-40077-8)

ALICE'S ADVENTURES IN WONDERLAND, Lewis Carroll. (0-486-27543-4)

THE CALL OF THE WILD, Jack London. (0-486-26472-6)

CRIME AND PUNISHMENT, Fyodor Dostoyevsky. Translated by Constance Garnett. (0-486-41587-2)

DRACULA, Bram Stoker. (0-486-41109-5)

ETHAN FROME, Edith Wharton. (0-486-26690-7)

FLATLAND, Edwin A. Abbott. (0-486-27263-X)

GREAT AMERICAN SHORT STORIES, Edited by Paul Negri. (0-486-42119-8)

GREAT EXPECTATIONS, Charles Dickens. (0-486-41586-4)

JANE EYRE, Charlotte Brontë. (0-486-42449-9)

THE JUNGLE, Upton Sinclair. (0-486-41923-1)

THE METAMORPHOSIS AND OTHER STORIES, Franz Kafka. (0-486-29030-1)

THE ODYSSEY, Homer. (0-486-40654-7)

THE PICTURE OF DORIAN GRAY, Oscar Wilde. (0-486-27807-7)

SIDDHARTHA, Hermann Hesse. (0-486-40653-9)

THE STRANGE CASE OF DR. JEKYLL AND MR. HYDE, Robert Louis Stevenson. (0-486-26688-5)

A TALE OF TWO CITIES, Charles Dickens. (0-486-40651-2)

WUTHERING HEIGHTS, Emily Brontë. (0-486-29256-8)

ANNA KARENINA, Leo Tolstoy. Translated by Louise and Aylmer Maude. (0-486-43796-5)

AROUND THE WORLD IN EIGHTY DAYS, Jules Verne. (0-486-41111-7)

THE BROTHERS KARAMAZOV, Fyodor Dostoyevsky. Translated by Constance Garnett. (0-486-43791-4)

CANDIDE, Voltaire. Edited by Francois-Marie Arouet. (0-486-26689-3)

DOVER · THRIFT · EDITIONS

FICTION

DAISY MILLER, Henry James. (0-486-28773-4)

DAVID COPPERFIELD, Charles Dickens. (0-486-43665-9)

DUBLINERS, James Joyce. (0-486-26870-5)

EMMA, Jane Austen. (0-486-40648-2)

THE GIFT OF THE MAGI AND OTHER SHORT STORIES, O. Henry. (0-486-27061-0)

THE GOLD-BUG AND OTHER TALES, Edgar Allan Poe. (0-486-26875-6)

GREAT SHORT SHORT STORIES, Edited by Paul Negri. (0-486-44098-2)

GULLIVER'S TRAVELS, Jonathan Swift. (0-486-29273-8)

HARD TIMES, Charles Dickens. (0-486-41920-7)

THE HOUND OF THE BASKERVILLES, Arthur Conan Doyle. (0-486-28214-7)

THE ILIAD, Homer. (0-486-40883-3)

MOBY-DICK, Herman Melville. (0-486-43215-7)

MY ÁNTONIA, Willa Cather. (0-486-28240-6)

NORTHANGER ABBEY, Jane Austen. (0-486-41412-4)

NOT WITHOUT LAUGHTER, Langston Hughes. (0-486-45448-7)

OLIVER TWIST, Charles Dickens. (0-486-42453-7)

PERSUASION, Jane Austen. (0-486-29555-9)

THE PHANTOM OF THE OPERA, Gaston Leroux. (0-486-43458-3)

A PORTRAIT OF THE ARTIST AS A YOUNG MAN, James Joyce. (0-486-28050-0)

PUDD'NHEAD WILSON, Mark Twain. (0-486-40885-X)

THE RED BADGE OF COURAGE, Stephen Crane. (0-486-26465-3)

THE SCARLET PIMPERNEL, Baroness Orczy. (0-486-42122-8)

SENSE AND SENSIBILITY, Jane Austen. (0-486-29049-2)

SILAS MARNER, George Eliot. (0-486-29246-0)

TESS OF THE D'URBERVILLES, Thomas Hardy. (0-486-41589-9)

THE TIME MACHINE, H. G. Wells. (0-486-28472-7)

TREASURE ISLAND, Robert Louis Stevenson. (0-486-27559-0)

THE TURN OF THE SCREW, Henry James. (0-486-26684-2)

UNCLE TOM'S CABIN, Harriet Beecher Stowe. (0-486-44028-1)

THE WAR OF THE WORLDS, H. G. Wells. (0-486-29506-0)

THE WORLD'S GREATEST SHORT STORIES, Edited by James Daley. (0-486-44716-2)

THE AGE OF INNOCENCE, Edith Wharton. (0-486-29803-5)

DOVER·THRIFT·EDITIONS

FICTION

AGNES GREY, Anne Brontë. (0-486-45121-6)

AT FAULT, Kate Chopin. (0-486-46133-5)

THE AUTOBIOGRAPHY OF AN EX-COLORED MAN, James Weldon Johnson. (0-486-28512-X)

BARTLEBY AND BENITO CERENO, Herman Melville. (0-486-26473-4)

BEOWULF, Translated by R. K. Gordon. (0-486-27264-8)

CIVIL WAR STORIES, Ambrose Bierce. (0-486-28038-1)

A CONNECTICUT YANKEE IN KING ARTHUR'S COURT, Mark Twain. (0-486-41591-0)

THE DEERSLAYER, James Fenimore Cooper. (0-486-46136-X)

DEMIAN, Hermann Hesse. (0-486-41413-2)

FAR FROM THE MADDING CROWD, Thomas Hardy. (0-486-45684-6)

FAVORITE FATHER BROWN STORIES, G. K. Chesterton. (0-486-27545-0)

GREAT HORROR STORIES, Edited by John Grafton. Introduction by Mike Ashley. (0-486-46143-2)

GREAT RUSSIAN SHORT STORIES, Edited by Paul Negri. (0-486-42992-X)

GREAT SHORT STORIES BY AMERICAN WOMEN, Edited by Candace Ward. (0-486-28776-9)

GRIMM'S FAIRY TALES, Jacob and Wilhelm Grimm. (0-486-45656-0)

HUMOROUS STORIES AND SKETCHES, Mark Twain. (0-486-29279-7)

THE HUNCHBACK OF NOTRE DAME, Victor Hugo. Translated by A. L. Alger. (0-486-45242-5)

THE INVISIBLE MAN, H. G. Wells. (0-486-27071-8)

THE ISLAND OF DR. MOREAU, H. G. Wells. (0-486-29027-1)

A JOURNAL OF THE PLAGUE YEAR, Daniel Defoe. (0-486-41919-3)

JOURNEY TO THE CENTER OF THE EARTH, Jules Verne. (0-486-44088-5)

KIM, Rudyard Kipling. (0-486-44508-9)

THE LAST OF THE MOHICANS, James Fenimore Cooper. (0-486-42678-5)

THE LEGEND OF SLEEPY HOLLOW AND OTHER STORIES, Washington Irving. (0-486-46658-2)

LILACS AND OTHER STORIES, Kate Chopin. (0-486-44095-8)

MANSFIELD PARK, Jane Austen. (0-486-41585-6)

THE MAYOR OF CASTERBRIDGE, Thomas Hardy. (0-486-43749-3)

THE MYSTERIOUS STRANGER AND OTHER STORIES, Mark Twain. (0-486-27069-6)

NOTES FROM THE UNDERGROUND, Fyodor Dostoyevsky. (0-486-27053-X)

DOVER · THRIFT · EDITIONS

FICTION

O PIONEERS!, Willa Cather. (0-486-27785-2)

AN OCCURRENCE AT OWL CREEK BRIDGE AND OTHER STORIES, Ambrose Bierce. (0-486-46657-4)

THE OLD CURIOSITY SHOP, Charles Dickens. (0-486-42679-3)

THE OPEN BOAT AND OTHER STORIES, Stephen Crane. (0-486-27547-7)

ROBINSON CRUSOE, Daniel Defoe. (0-486-40427-7)

THIS SIDE OF PARADISE, F. Scott Fitzgerald. (0-486-28999-0)

THE THREE MUSKETEERS, Alexandre Dumas. (0-486-45681-1)

TWENTY THOUSAND LEAGUES UNDER THE SEA, Jules Verne. (0-486-44849-5)

WHITE FANG, Jack London. (0-486-26968-X)

WHITE NIGHTS AND OTHER STORIES, Fyodor Dostoyevsky. (0-486-46948-4)

NONFICTION

GREAT SPEECHES, Abraham Lincoln. (0-486-26872-1)

WISDOM OF THE BUDDHA, Edited by F. Max Müller. (0-486-41120-6)

NARRATIVE OF SOJOURNER TRUTH, Sojourner Truth. (0-486-29899-X)

THE TRIAL AND DEATH OF SOCRATES, Plato. (0-486-27066-1)

WIT AND WISDOM OF THE AMERICAN PRESIDENTS, Edited by Joslyn Pine. (0-486-41427-2)

GREAT SPEECHES BY AFRICAN AMERICANS, Edited by James Daley. (0-486-44761-8)

INTERIOR CASTLE, St. Teresa of Avila. Edited and Translated by E. Allison Peers. (0-486-46145-9)

GREAT SPEECHES BY AMERICAN WOMEN, Edited by James Daley. (0-486-46141-6)

ON LIBERTY, John Stuart Mill. (0-486-42130-9)

MEDITATIONS, Marcus Aurelius. (0-486-29823-X)

THE SOULS OF BLACK FOLK, W.E.B. DuBois. (0-486-28041-1)

GREAT SPEECHES BY NATIVE AMERICANS, Edited by Bob Blaisdell. (0-486-41122-2)

WIT AND WISDOM FROM POOR RICHARD'S ALMANACK, Benjamin Franklin. (0-486-40891-4)

THE AUTOBIOGRAPHY OF BENJAMIN FRANKLIN, Benjamin Franklin. (0-486-29073-5)

OSCAR WILDE'S WIT AND WISDOM, Oscar Wilde. (0-486-40146-4)

THE WIT AND WISDOM OF ABRAHAM LINCOLN, Abraham Lincoln. Edited by Bob Blaisdell. (0-486-44097-4)

DOVER · THRIFT · EDITIONS

NONFICTION

ON THE ORIGIN OF SPECIES, Charles Darwin. (0-486-45006-6)

SIX GREAT DIALOGUES, Plato. Translated by Benjamin Jowett. (0-486-45465-7)

NATURE AND OTHER ESSAYS, Ralph Waldo Emerson. (0-486-46947-6)

THE COMMUNIST MANIFESTO AND OTHER REVOLUTIONARY WRITINGS, Edited by Bob Blaisdell. (0-486-42465-0)

THE CONFESSIONS OF ST. AUGUSTINE, St. Augustine. (0-486-42466-9)

THE WIT AND WISDOM OF MARK TWAIN, Mark Twain. (0-486-40664-4)

LIFE ON THE MISSISSIPPI, Mark Twain. (0-486-41426-4)

BEYOND GOOD AND EVIL, Friedrich Nietzsche. (0-486-29868-X)

CIVIL DISOBEDIENCE AND OTHER ESSAYS, Henry David Thoreau. (0-486-27563-9)

A MODEST PROPOSAL AND OTHER SATIRICAL WORKS, Jonathan Swift. (0-486-28759-9)

UTOPIA, Sir Thomas More. (0-486-29583-4)

GREAT SPEECHES, Franklin Delano Roosevelt. (0-486-40894-9)

WALDEN; OR, LIFE IN THE WOODS, Henry David Thoreau. (0-486-28495-6)

UP FROM SLAVERY, Booker T. Washington. (0-486-28738-6)

DARK NIGHT OF THE SOUL, St. John of the Cross. (0-486-42693-9)

GREEK AND ROMAN LIVES, Plutarch. Translated by John Dryden. Revised and Edited by Arthur Hugh Clough. (0-486-44576-3)

WOMEN'S WIT AND WISDOM, Edited by Susan L. Rattiner. (0-486-41123-0)

MUSIC, Edited by Herb Galewitz. (0-486-41596-1)

INCIDENTS IN THE LIFE OF A SLAVE GIRL, Harriet Jacobs. (0-486-41931-2)

THE LIFE OF OLAUDAH EQUIANO, Olaudah Equiano. (0-486-40661-X)

THE DECLARATION OF INDEPENDENCE AND OTHER GREAT DOCUMENTS OF AMERICAN HISTORY, Edited by John Grafton. (0-486-41124-9)

THE PRINCE, Niccolò Machiavelli. (0-486-27274-5)

WOMAN IN THE NINETEENTH CENTURY, Margaret Fuller. (0-486-40662-8)

SELF-RELIANCE AND OTHER ESSAYS, Ralph Waldo Emerson. (0-486-27790-9)

COMMON SENSE, Thomas Paine. (0-486-29602-4)

THE REPUBLIC, Plato. (0-486-41121-4)

POETICS, Aristotle. (0-486-29577-X)

THE DEVIL'S DICTIONARY, Ambrose Bierce. (0-486-27542-6)

NARRATIVE OF THE LIFE OF FREDERICK DOUGLASS, Frederick Douglass. (0-486-28499-9)

DOVER · THRIFT · EDITIONS

NONFICTION

GREAT ENGLISH ESSAYS, Edited by Bob Blaisdell. (0-486-44082-6)

THE KORAN, Translated by J. M. Rodwell. (0-486-44569-0)

28 GREAT INAUGURAL ADDRESSES, Edited by John Grafton and James Daley. (0-486-44621-2)

WHEN I WAS A SLAVE, Edited by Norman R. Yetman. (0-486-42070-1)

THE IMITATION OF CHRIST, Thomas à Kempis. Translated by Aloysius Croft and Harold Bolton. (0-486-43185-1)

PLAYS

ANTIGONE, Sophocles. (0-486-27804-2)

AS YOU LIKE IT, William Shakespeare. (0-486-40432-3)

CYRANO DE BERGERAC, Edmond Rostand. (0-486-41119-2)

A DOLL'S HOUSE, Henrik Ibsen. (0-486-27062-9)

DR. FAUSTUS, Christopher Marlowe. (0-486-28208-2)

FIVE COMIC ONE-ACT PLAYS, Anton Chekhov. (0-486-40887-6)

FIVE GREAT COMEDIES, William Shakespeare. (0-486-44086-9)

FIVE GREAT GREEK TRAGEDIES, Sophocles, Euripides and Aeschylus. (0-486-43620-9)

FOUR GREAT HISTORIES, William Shakespeare. (0-486-44629-8)

FOUR GREAT RUSSIAN PLAYS, Anton Chekhov, Nikolai Gogol, Maxim Gorky, and Ivan Turgenev. (0-486-43472-9)

FOUR GREAT TRAGEDIES, William Shakespeare. (0-486-44083-4)

GHOSTS, Henrik Ibsen. (0-486-29852-3)

HAMLET, William Shakespeare. (0-486-27278-8)

HENRY V, William Shakespeare. (0-486-42887-7)

AN IDEAL HUSBAND, Oscar Wilde. (0-486-41423-X)

THE IMPORTANCE OF BEING EARNEST, Oscar Wilde. (0-486-26478-5)

JULIUS CAESAR, William Shakespeare. (0-486-26876-4)

KING LEAR, William Shakespeare. (0-486-28058-6)

LOVE'S LABOUR'S LOST, William Shakespeare. (0-486-41929-0)

LYSISTRATA, Aristophanes. (0-486-28225-2)

MACBETH, William Shakespeare. (0-486-27802-6)

MAJOR BARBARA, George Bernard Shaw. (0-486-42126-0)

MEDEA, Euripides. (0-486-27548-5)

DOVER·THRIFT·EDITIONS

PLAYS

THE MERCHANT OF VENICE, William Shakespeare. (0-486-28492-1)

A MIDSUMMER NIGHT'S DREAM, William Shakespeare. (0-486-27067-X)

MUCH ADO ABOUT NOTHING, William Shakespeare. (0-486-28272-4)

OEDIPUS REX, Sophocles. (0-486-26877-2)

THE ORESTEIA TRILOGY, Aeschylus. (0-486-29242-8)

OTHELLO, William Shakespeare. (0-486-29097-2)

THE PLAYBOY OF THE WESTERN WORLD AND RIDERS TO THE SEA, J. M. Synge. (0-486-27562-0)

PYGMALION, George Bernard Shaw. (0-486-28222-8)

ROMEO AND JULIET, William Shakespeare. (0-486-27557-4)

THE TAMING OF THE SHREW, William Shakespeare. (0-486-29765-9)

TARTUFFE, Molière. (0-486-41117-6)

THE TEMPEST, William Shakespeare. (0-486-40658-X)

TWELFTH NIGHT; OR, WHAT YOU WILL, William Shakespeare. (0-486-29290-8)

RICHARD III, William Shakespeare. (0-486-28747-5)

HEDDA GABLER, Henrik Ibsen. (0-486-26469-6)

THE COMEDY OF ERRORS, William Shakespeare. (0-486-42461-8)

THE CHERRY ORCHARD, Anton Chekhov. (0-486-26682-6)

SHE STOOPS TO CONQUER, Oliver Goldsmith. (0-486-26867-5)

THE WILD DUCK, Henrik Ibsen. (0-486-41116-8)

THE WINTER'S TALE, William Shakespeare. (0-486-41118-4)

ARMS AND THE MAN, George Bernard Shaw. (0-486-26476-9)

EVERYMAN, Anonymous. (0-486-28726-2)

THE FATHER, August Strindberg. (0-486-43217-3)

R.U.R., Karel Capek. (0-486-41926-6)

THE BEGGAR'S OPERA, John Gay. (0-486-40888-4)

3 BY SHAKESPEARE, William Shakespeare. (0-486-44721-9)

PROMETHEUS BOUND, Aeschylus. (0-486-28762-9)